HOLLY HILLS CHRISTMAS

A.D. ELLIS

ONE
DAKOTA "KOTA" SCOTT

"NO, NO, NO," I muttered as I pumped the brakes and did my best to steer into the slide. But it was no use, my car careened through the slick, icy snow and came to rest half on, half off the tiny but steep uphill road to Holly Hills. Slamming my hand against the steering wheel, I took a deep breath in hopes of calming myself. It didn't work. "Fuck, fuck, *fuck.*"

I put my car in Park and thumped my head onto the headrest.

Just what I needed.

Not.

As if my week hadn't already been bad enough. Hell, my entire month had been less than stellar. And now, on the way to Holly Hills to visit my dying grandmother as her last wish, I get stuck on the side of the road in a damn snowstorm.

Fan-fucking-tastic.

The snow had been falling steadily before I headed toward Holly Hills, the small town known for celebrating the joy of Christmas all year, but I was used to snow in the winter after living in the Midwest my entire life. I hadn't been too worried as I pointed my car south.

However, the snow had increased with each passing minute on my four-hour drive and I'd grown increasingly concerned the closer I got to Holly Hills. I'd known I was pushing my luck to keep going, but if I could just get up the final hill, I'd be safe and warm in Grandma Mary Joy's kitchen at the Amaryllis Inn.

Yes, her given name was Mary Joy.

Yes, she ran the Holly Hills bed-and-breakfast which was named after a Christmas flower.

Yes, I'd left the city to take part in what was quickly turning into a holiday-themed nightmare.

But in all honesty, it sounded somewhat better than what I'd left behind, so maybe it wouldn't be *all* that bad.

Sadly, the snowstorm was a wicked beast and had me in its clutches. A layer of ice had been put down first, followed by what seemed to be about six to eight inches of heavy, wet snow—a lot more had fallen here than four hours north—and another round of icy sleet pelted at my windows. The mixed layers plus the steep hill had been my downfall for sure.

I pulled out my phone, knowing there'd be no signal, but hoping all the same.

Nope. Nothing. Nada.

It was the same thing every time I came to visit Grandma. I'd have service most of the drive, then once I reached the smaller hills and valleys below Holly Hills, I'd lose all signal. Once I got to the very top of the monstrosity where Holly Hills sat, my bars would return like magic.

Granted, I hadn't been to visit Mary Joy in a couple years, but I assumed cell service at the base of the hill was still zero and the snowstorm wasn't helping anything. I could only hope service would be better once I got to the hilltop.

If I got to the hilltop.

Fuck.

I leaned forward and rested my head on the steering wheel.

I was no stranger to driving in snow. Maybe I could get a bit of traction and reverse my way out of the ditch. I put the car in gear. The snow laughed and called me a bitch while my tires spun in the icy mess.

Because, of course.

If no one came along soon, I'd need to get out and make sure no snow was blocking my tailpipe. The last thing I needed to add to my shitty month was dying of asphyxiation. I could sit in the warm car for as long as my gas held out; I had water and snacks. But eventually, I'd have to trek my way up the hill. Luckily, I had a warm winter coat, but the comfy sports slides I'd opted to wear on the drive weren't optimal for snowy conditions.

Fuck.

Why had I even decided to come to Holly Hills to spend time with Grandma Mary Joy? A stab of guilty pain jolted me from my little pity party as I recalled the words of her last letter to me—yes, Mary Joy was a spunky, kindhearted, opinionated eighty-year-old spitfire who kept up her end of what was possibly a one-woman campaign to save the art of letter writing.

Kota Christopher,

I hope this letter finds you well. How is that fancy job treating you? Your mom and dad were so very proud of you landing such a top-notch position at that company. They tell me it's one of the very best in your field. I hope you're happy there for many years to come.

How's that man of yours? What's his name? Forgive me, I'm old. Mitch? Mike? Matt? Anyway, is he a nice boy? Are you serious about him? Will there be a Holly Hills wedding in the future?

Although, speaking of the future of Holly Hills, I'll be honest and say I'm worried. Each year gets a bit more challenging. With my health failing, I sometimes wonder if this will be the year that ends it all. Will I even live to see another Holly Hills Christmas with the Amaryllis Inn packed full of happy guests?

If I were given one last wish, it would be to have my only grandson with me this season. I know you're terribly busy with your big, important job—an old lady and her small hilltop bed-and-breakfast can't possibly compete with that—but a girl can dream, right?

I know your parents are traveling this holiday, so know you've always got a place here at Holly Hills if you're hankering for a family holiday.

Love,

Grandma Mary Joy

I swallowed thickly and tried not to think about the words *failing health* and *last wish*. Hell, she was the only grandparent I'd known for most of my life. My maternal grandparents had both passed before I was born and my paternal grandfather had died when I was just a baby. Grandma Mary Joy had showered me with gifts and affection and spoiled me rotten when we lived closer. After I moved away for college, our visits got fewer and farther between, but we still kept in touch.

As for the job she mentioned, my conflicted heart wasn't sure if it should soar or sink. I'd landed a graphics design position at one of the most high-paying, upscale advertising firms in the region right after college.

Only to find that I absolutely abhorred the place.

Talk about a punch to the gut. Spending four years in college learning everything I could about graphic design and getting what I thought was my dream job, then quickly realizing that the company was a place where souls went to die.

Sure, they paid a lot, but that was likely just to keep people around. They were sought after, and they *did* do good work, but it was one of the most negative, soul-sucking, isolating, and demeaning places I'd ever stepped foot into. The people ranged from hateful, detached, unreasonable, uncaring management to zombie-like, cut-throat, nasty lackeys who would seriously do *anything* to get named to a project. I'm sure there were top-level executives, but the low-lifes never saw them.

So, had I felt bummed when they called me in and told me they were letting me go? Yeah, a bit. Their reasoning was that I wasn't showing the competitive drive they'd hoped to nurture in me.

What they'd *meant* was I wasn't a dick willing to screw over my colleagues and anyone else while doing mind-numbingly boring work for clients I had absolutely no contact with.

That wasn't why I'd gotten into graphic design. I loved art of all kinds and I wanted more than anything to see my work on ads, but I also wanted to see it on greeting cards, in magazines and books, maybe even in movies.

I wanted to think I'd eventually get there, and losing my job wasn't the greatest move on my part, but I knew I'd never get where I wanted to be in my career if I lost my soul to that dreadful company.

So, yeah, I'd need to tell Mary Joy that I was jobless. The one bright spot was they'd paid me *very* well and I'd saved a large portion of my income, plus they'd offered me a severance package—I think it was mainly hush money so I'd hopefully not tell others how terrible they were—so I wasn't destitute.

I winced.

While not destitute, I *was* technically homeless.

Sighing heavily as the snow and sleet continued to pelt my windows, I recalled the late November conversation with my three roommates. They'd all opted to go their separate ways once our lease was up in December since our rent was increasing and they all had friends or partners to move in with. Which had left me with a quadruple rent *or* moving out as well.

Obviously, I'd opted to move out. The apartment wasn't that great and I had no desire to try to find three new roommates.

So, Mary Joy's invite to Holly Hills had come at the perfect time since I needed a place to stay.

As for Mike...

I sighed again.

Mike was a great guy. We'd been friends all through college and got along great. Somewhere along the line, we'd decided that maybe our friendship could be something more. For a while, it was good. And by *a while*, I mean like a week. But then I'd realized the sex was good and I loved the guy, but I wasn't *in love* with him and the sex wasn't the kind that curled your toes or sent shockwaves through your body—honestly, did that type of sex even exist in real life?

Mike and I had given in to loneliness and found out that *sometimes* best friends fall head-over-heels in love and *sometimes* best friends start having sex for the sake of having sex and realize it was probably a really dumb decision.

Which was why I wasn't shocked or upset when Mike sheepishly told me he'd met someone at his bar job and asked if I'd be terribly pissed to give up my ticket for the cruise he'd invited me to go on.

I mean, on one hand, I probably should have been upset. My best friend had invited me to go on a cruise—the invite had come before we'd added sex into the equation, if that matters—and then he'd pretty much dumped my ass for some new pretty-boy *and* took away my chance at a tropical island paradise just so he could get some ass. Ass that wasn't mine.

But honestly, the sparkle in Mike's eyes when he talked

about this guy was exactly what had been missing between us and I knew I couldn't argue if he wanted to take a trip with his new man.

Thing was, I wasn't even jealous or hurt. Mike and I had agreed to the safe-sex-always rule along with being okay if we saw other people. Which, in hindsight, was another red flag that we were meant only for friendship because I couldn't see myself being okay with a man I was in love with sleeping with others. No judgement for those who do, it just wasn't for me.

"Let's recap," I said to the empty car and chuckled. I might have been starting to go a bit crazy. "Kota Scott—who is now talking about himself in third person—is a twenty-four-year old with no job, no home, and no boyfriend. He's found himself stuck in a snowstorm on the way to visit fucking Holly Jolly Christmas Town in hopes of brightening his dying grandmother's remaining time and spending a holiday at one of the places that brought him the most joy as a child." I slow-clapped. "He's a catch, ladies and gentlemen, a real catch."

Fighting the urge to both giggle like a maniac and cry my eyes out, I thumped my head back. Holly Hills really was one of my favorite places as a kid. But as a grown man who'd lost his job, his apartment, and his friend-with-benefits all in the last month, the thought of being joyous or finding happiness in a perpetual Christmas town was a bit daunting.

Taking a deep breath, I steeled myself for what was ahead.

First, I'd check the tailpipe.

Next, I'd warm up in the car a bit.

Then, I'd climb my lean ass—slip-on shoes and all—up the damn icy hill and find Mary Joy.

Maybe it was time to push aside my own problems and focus on someone else. My grandmother requested me to spend one last holiday season with her as her dying wish. I

could help with the bed-and-breakfast, maybe do a little
artwork, and make an old woman happy.

If I was lucky, the time I spent at Holly Hills would give
me some sort of direction as to where I needed to go next in
life.

As I mentally prepared for the inevitable icy-cold hell I
was about to face, I took three deep breaths and did my best
to convince myself that a little cold wouldn't kill me.

I'm not ashamed to admit I screamed like a child when a
knock sounded to my left. The dark figure outside my
window knocked again and bent down to peer through the
icy glass.

"Please, please, please let the magic of all things
Christmas surround me and have this person be friend, not
foe," I muttered to myself. Yeah, I was about three seconds
from complete crazy-town. I needed a warm fire, hot
chocolate, and Mary Joy's homemade meals to bring me back
to reality.

With one last silent prayer that the hulking figure
belonged to a gentle giant, I cracked my window and offered
a smile.

"Good day, kind sir," I said solemnly, right before
laughing like a loon for mere moments before tears streamed
down my face.

Fan-fucking-tastic.

TWO

ALAN VINCENT "VINCE" CARTER

HOLY HELL.

I'd come down the hill to do a sweep for anyone not able to make it up the steep incline and found a beautiful blond-haired, blue-eyed angel who appeared to be on the edge of a breakdown.

Shit.

The kid looked scared, exhausted, and totally done-in. I knew my large frame, made even larger by the bulky winter-wear, was intimidating to some, so I knelt down to bring myself more to his eye level.

He gave a final hiccupping sob before dashing tears away with the back of his hands and rolling the window down a bit farther. "I'm so sorry. I don't usually act like a crazy person."

I smiled, not sure how much of it he could see with my face mostly covered. "I'm Vince Carter, I live up the hill. Is that where you're headed?"

The kid nodded. I guess *kid* wasn't right, he looked to be on the lower side of his mid-twenties. But at forty-four, I saw pretty much anyone younger than thirty-five as a kid.

"I'm Dakota Scott. I'm staying at my grandmother's bed-and-breakfast."

Holy shit.

This was Mary Joy's grandson?

Wait, what? Staying at the Amaryllis? That couldn't be right.

I cleared my throat but bit back my reply. "Let's get you up the hill. Mary Joy will be thrilled to see you."

Dakota's eyes lit up. "You know my grandma?"

Quirking an eyebrow, I chuckled. "It's a town of well under a thousand and she owns the inn. Pretty sure everyone knows Mary Joy."

He glanced in his mirror. "Is that your truck?" Then he rubbed his brow. "Of course, it's your truck. You didn't just appear out of thin air. Can your truck get me unstuck?"

I winced. "Well, the good news is yes, I can eventually get your car out."

Dakota eyed me warily. "And the bad news?"

I shrugged, my shoulders heavy in the massive coat. "It won't be until the storm stops and the roads get cleared." I glanced around and realized the snow fall rate had increased and visibility was next-to-nothing. "Now, I don't mean to be pushy, but we really need to get my truck up this hill or we're both going to be stuck down here. And no one else is coming down, I can promise you that."

Dakota's eyes went wide and he scrambled to gather his belongings.

"You got bags in the back?" I asked. "Pop the trunk," I said when he nodded.

We made short work of tossing his stuff in the truck and I said a quick little prayer that my snow tires would get us up to Holly Hills.

Despite the terrible weather and road conditions, Dakota

seemed to be a talker. "How long have you lived in Holly Hills?"

"Couple years," I said, doing my best to keep the truck on the road as the incline got steeper. I usually didn't find myself interested in chit-chat, but something about Dakota loosened my lips.

"I used to come here all the time to visit Grandma, loved it as a kid. How is she?"

I cursed under my breath as the truck slid a bit, but chuckled at his question. "Oh, you know Mary Joy. Spitfire as usual."

Dakota frowned slightly. "I hope I can make this season good for her. What do you do in town?"

"Little bit of everything. I moved to get away from…" I paused, I wasn't spilling my whole life story to this kid five minutes after I met him, no matter how much he made me want to talk. "Just to get away from the big city and all the stress of my old job. I didn't plan on coming to Holly Hills or staying—Christmas isn't really my thing—but the place stuck its claws in me and I couldn't leave. I teach art classes after school, I do odds and ends jobs around town, and I help Mary Joy with the property."

"Wow, you sure your name isn't Jack?"

When I tossed him a confused look, Dakota shrugged. "You know, *Jack of all trades*? Never mind. Why is Christmas not your thing?"

Now it was my turn to shrug. "My parents were super religious growing up and *I* was super gay." Normally, I wouldn't toss out my sexuality to a complete stranger, but I knew Mary Joy's grandson was gay, so it felt safe. "They, and their church, turned me off anything remotely religious. Christmas was one of the big holidays where I'd get constant lectures and reminders of how much of a sinner I was and how I needed to turn from my evil ways. I moved out when I was sixteen and lived with an aunt, things got a lot better then. But I still have aversions to anything religious, even though I know not all religions and the people who practice are homophobic. Christmas just left a bad taste in my mouth —a reminder of how my parents chose a religion over me."

"Wow, I'm sorry. I lucked out that my parents took me being gay pretty much in stride. I'm an only child and I was left on my own a lot. Not like neglected, just raised to be independent. Mom and Dad travel more than they're home. I told them I was gay, they hugged me, checked their flight time, and headed out again." Dakota wiped at the frosty window. "I can see why religious holidays might not be your thing. But Christmas is so commercialized these days, sometimes it's easy to forget it's not just about Santa and presents."

"Even harder to forget when you live in a Christmas town," I said as the truck crested the last bit of the hill.

"I bet," Dakota said with a laugh. "Thanks so much for rescuing me. How did you know I was down there?" He shivered, probably from the cold *and* his stressful drive.

"Didn't know. Just went on a final sweep to see if anyone had been…" I paused. Shit, I couldn't call the kid dumb.

"Stupid enough to try the Holly Hills hill in a snowstorm?" Dakota deadpanned. "Ding, ding, ding! I'm the winner." He waved off my protest. "No, I should have known better than to attempt that hill. I just wanted to see Mary Joy and get some good food in front of the fire. Maybe some hot chocolate and cookies. I've had a shit few weeks and I was desperate, but it *was* dumb to try that hill. Thank you."

I bypassed the Amaryllis Inn's front entrance and headed toward the guest house which was located about a mile from the bed-and-breakfast.

"Wait, you missed the turn. I'm going to the inn to see Mary Joy."

I gritted my teeth. Had the old lady not told him? Shit.

"The inn is packed full. Mary Joy has you staying at the guest house."

Dakota frowned. "Oh, well, can we at least stop to say hi?"

"Sorry, can't. This whole town—hell, the whole county—is about five minutes from shutting down from this storm. We'll be lucky if we can make the final turn to the house without getting stuck. Once the snow stops, I'll use the utility vehicle to take you to her. Knowing her, though, she'll demand I bring her to you. As long as the power holds, you should be good to FaceTime her if she's not too busy."

I pulled the truck around the final turn and breathed a sigh of relief as we slid to a stop in front of the house.

"Too busy? She's not doing it all by herself is she? I'm glad she has guests—that should help, right? But is she in any condition to work like that?" Dakota asked.

"She's got a couple girls from town who said they'd stay on during these next few weeks leading up to Christmas." I put the truck into Park. "She's not doing it alone. Once the town opens back up, you can come and go as you please and help her too."

Dakota huffed. "Okay. I just feel bad. I came to see her and help and I'm stuck a mile away."

"Yeah, Old Man Winter doesn't give two shits about our plans most of the time."

"Well, thanks for the ride. Are you going to be able to make it home?" Dakota asked as he reached for the door handle.

I closed my eyes and sighed. "Um, I live here. Mary Joy lets me stay in exchange for working for her. Since the inn is bursting at the seams, she asked me if it was okay that you stay here too."

Dakota's eyes went wide. "Oh, wow. Um, okay. Cool. Thanks for letting me invade your space."

"It's no problem. Least I can do for her. Hop out. I'm going to get the truck in the garage and bring your bags." I pointed toward the porch. "I'll meet you at the door."

Dakota nodded and climbed from the truck, his blond hair quickly covered in icy flakes as he made his way through knee-high snow.

Shit. I wasn't in the place to deny the kid a warm place to stay, but did he have to be so damn cute? No way I could go getting involved with Mary Joy's grandson. He wasn't even going to stay—I'd heard he had a big, fancy city job to get back to.

A short and sweet holiday fling may be just what you need.

No. I wasn't getting messed up in that type of situation again. I'd moved on from my city life of having a different guy in my bed every weekend. I'd learned my lesson about sleeping with a friend's family member—that fiasco had been what ended my very public career as a big-name art critic and landed me in the middle of nowhere. I shook my head as I grabbed Dakota's bags, closed the garage door, and headed toward the house. What I *needed* was to continue living an uncomplicated life of solitude.

I was happy.

Mostly.

This place was good for me.

So what if I got pangs of loneliness from time-to-time? I liked what I did in Holly Hills. The whole Christmas theme was a bit much, but it didn't stop me from enjoying my new life. I had my art classes, which were actually a ton more fun than I ever would have dreamed. I enjoyed helping out around town with small jobs. And I was able to keep my hand in the big world of art by doing critiques online and writing for a select few publications.

I was *Vince* to the people of Holly Hills, but I was still Alan Vincent, Art Critic, to the art snobs of the world. I hadn't done the math, but I figured I actually had more requests for critiques and interviews once I'd disappeared from my old life than I'd had when I was in the public eye.

My life in Holly Hills was good and I didn't need to get involved with my friend's grandson just because I was lonely and had an itch.

Plus, I definitely wasn't one to believe in the magic of Christmas or whatever. This situation wasn't a holiday movie with some grand love story. It was just real life and real life was never as good as fiction.

Dakota Scott was here to visit his grandmother, help out a bit to make himself feel better, and then say goodbye without a second glance as he headed back north to his big city job and boyfriend.

If I was smart, I'd keep all of that in mind. I'd forget all about his pretty blue eyes and pink rosy cheeks. I'd forget the strange draw the kid seemed to have on me.

I could hear fate laughing at me as I climbed the stairs to find a shivering cold and very snow-covered Dakota on the porch.

"My coat is great, my lounge pants and sports slides with socks, not so much." His teeth chattered as he spoke.

"Let's get you inside. I'll get a fire going and you can change clothes. We'll see if the WiFi is working and you can FaceTime Mary Joy."

Once inside, I sent Dakota down the hall to the unoccupied bedroom to change into dry clothes.

A few minutes later, wondering what he wanted to drink, I stepped into the hallway and hollered, "Dakota? Coffee, tea, or hot chocolate?"

No answer.

I hadn't heard the shower turn on. Shit, had the kid already conked out?

I walked farther down the hall. "Dakota?"

"You can call me Kota," he mumbled as I came around the doorframe and found him standing in the middle of the bedroom.

"Kota," I murmured, tasting his name on my tongue and loving its flavor. I stood next to him and tried to figure out what was wrong.

Wait. What *was* wrong? Something was off.

"Um, I don't mind sleeping on the floor at all, but why is there no bed in here?" Kota asked.

No bed? What?

"Why is there no bed in here?" I repeated like an idiot. "I have absolutely no clue. I don't come in here often, but I would have sworn there was a bed when I left here this morning." Was I losing my mind? I *knew* there had been a bed in this room at some point. But now, it was just a large room with a bare space where a bed used to be.

If Kota hadn't been seeing the same thing as me, I would have wondered if I was hallucinating. Maybe I'd gotten too cold outside and I was experiencing shock or something.

"No worries, I can sleep on the couch," Kota said. "Can I shower and then get a hot chocolate?"

"Definitely, and don't ask for permission, this house is more yours than mine," I answered, still staring at where his bed *should* have been. "The kitchen is stocked to last us a week or more, we'll have some dinner in a bit."

Kota gave me a grateful, tired smile as I headed back to the kitchen. I set to work making hot chocolate for him and coffee for me as I gathered a small tray of fruit, meat, crackers, and cheese. I figured he'd want to talk to Mary Joy for a bit, but he was likely hungry after driving through such heavy snow and getting stuck.

Kota came around the corner a bit later and smiled. "I feel so much better. Amazing what being dry and warm can do for a person. Can I help?"

"Grab the mugs," I said as I picked up the tray of food and the iPad. "We can make a fire in the living room and call your grandma."

I nearly slammed into Kota's back when he came to a dead stop as he rounded the corner into the living room. "Shit, sorry," I muttered.

"Uh, Vince?" Kota's voice had me instantly concerned.

I stepped around him and cursed.

The couch was gone.

"What in the ever lovin' fuck..." I growled under my breath. "You're seeing this, right? There's no couch? Or am I losing my mind?"

"No couch. Nice big pile of blankets and pillows, but no couch." Kota turned toward me. "It was here this morning?"

"I know for sure it was here. I fell asleep out here last night and woke with a crick in my neck this morning." I put the food on the coffee table and went to work building a fire. "Let's get this going and we'll call Mary Joy. See if she knows what's going on. I don't think we were robbed since nothing else seems to be missing. Plus, no one in town would steal from Mary Joy and any outsiders wouldn't have been able to get up the hill or out of here with a bed and a couch without being noticed."

We settled in on the blankets and pillows—which I thought had probably come from the ample supply in the closet and attic room—and took a couple minutes to enjoy our drinks and snacks.

"How bad is she?" Kota asked as he nibbled on a cracker.

"Huh?"

"Mary Joy, is she bad? Her health?"

I frowned. "Her health is fine, why?"

Now it was Kota's turn to frown. "Fine? What do you mean, fine? Her health is failing and she asked me here as her dying wish."

My eyes went wide. "I don't pretend to know her more than her own grandson, but just yesterday she walked a mile with a couple other ladies and they went for a swim at the rec center. If she's failing, she's going a good job of hiding it."

"What the hell is she up to?" Kota muttered.

"Let's see what she has to say," I offered and opened the iPad to make the call.

"Kota Christopher," Mary Joy crowed as the call connected. "As I live and breathe, you're really here?" She peered at the screen, adjusting her device as she spoke.

Kota chuckled. "I'm here. Barely made it. My car went off the road at the bottom of the hill. Vince rescued me."

"Well, land's sakes, I'm glad I didn't know about that or I'd have been worried sick." She smiled broadly, a dishtowel hung over her shoulder as she seemed to multitask while working in the kitchen. "I'm just so glad to have you here. Now, you'll have to be patient as we wait out this storm. It's not supposed to stop until tomorrow and then it'll take a while until the town opens back up. I'd think Vince can probably haul my skinny butt over on the utility cart in a day or two."

I scooted closer and popped my face on the screen. "Maybe I'll see about bringing Kota to you before I try to taxi you in the icy cold."

"Oh, don't you two just look comfy cozy? I'm so sorry I couldn't be there to greet you, but I'm up to my elbows in guests and dinner." Mary Joy gave a wink before turning to speak to someone next to her, her long silver hair pulled up in its usual bun and her plump cheeks pink with happiness. "Vince, thank you, dear. For getting my Kota up the hill and sharing your space with him. I just know you boys will settle in together nicely and be the best of friends."

Kota cleared his throat and I caught the faint hint of a blush on his cheeks.

Was Mary Joy matchmaking?

"Mary Joy," I leaned closer to Kota again so she could see me. "Would you happen to know where the couch and the spare bed took off to?" It wasn't *that* unusual for Mary Joy to take things from the house and use them at the inn. But she usually took things like plates, blankets, or a slow-cooker, not entire pieces of furniture.

Mary Joy stepped away from the screen and we heard her giving directions about linens and coffee and the cleaning of toilets before she came back into view. "Oh yes, dear, I'm sorry I didn't have time to tell you. With the storm coming in and the BnB filling up so quickly, I really wasn't thinking."

We waited a beat, but she didn't continue.

"Where are the couch and bed?" Kota asked.

"Oh, yes, they were desperately needed here at the inn. I'll get them returned at some point. I apologize for any inconvenience, but the business was in need. I'm sure you two will figure out a way to make it work." She glanced away from the screen, clearly somewhat distracted with the goings-on at the inn.

"Had I known I needed to sleep on the floor, I would have brought an air mattress," Kota grumbled, sounding a bit like a petulant child.

"Poppycock," Mary Joy declared. "No one needs to sleep on the floor. Your grandfather Kris and I spent many *very* happy years in that large king-sized bed. It's basically the size of the Sahara. Plenty of room, but also great for cuddling on a cold winter night."

Kota made a strangled noise.

Shit.

She was definitely matchmaking.

"Vince, how's the plant I gave you?" Mary Joy asked.

Double shit.

"Oh, um, it's seen better days," I said with a wince.

"No worries, I have faith. With the right amount of love and Christmas magic, it will come around. And then you'll see you don't have be such a Grinch." Mary Joy moved away from the camera again before popping back into view. "I only have a moment before I'll have to say goodbye."

"Grandma, I'm happy to be here, but why did you make me think the Amaryllis was about to close down and you were dying?" Kota asked, quirking his brow.

Mary Joy's eyes went wide. "I did no such thing, Kota Christopher," she sputtered.

Kota blew out a breath. "Your letter said you worried this would be the last year for the inn, you talked about your failing health, and said if you had one last wish it would be to have me here. I drove here thinking I was going to find you on your deathbed, not stealing furniture and dispensing Christmas flowers."

"Stuff and nonsense," Mary Joy declared with a wave of her hand. "Every year *could* be the last for the Amaryllis, but it won't be this year. We're not in some Hallmark movie where the long-lost family member comes home to save the failing business."

"What about your health and your last wish?" Kota pressed.

"I'm fit as a fiddle," Mary Joy argued.

"Then why did you mention your failing health?" Kota was clearly frustrated.

She waved her hand again. "I'm eighty, I'm allowed to have bad days. I have a bunion that acts up from time-to-time and my back isn't what it used to be. Doctor says I likely have a good bit of arthritis, my eyes will never be twenty-

twenty, and I need more fiber in my diet to keep things moving, but I'm alive and well. I was probably just being maudlin and missing my grandson." Mary Joy glanced away and nodded. "I've gotta go. The inn filled up quickly with travelers looking to avoid the storm and we're booked solid for the week and through the month. We'll chat soon. I need a hug."

And with that, she ended to call.

THREE

KOTA

"OH MY GOD." I flopped back on the pile of blankets and pillows. "I love her dearly, but that was one of the most exasperating conversations I've ever had."

Vince nodded. "I'm sorry there was such a misunderstanding. Maybe she thought you wouldn't come if she told you everything was fine?"

I winced. "Yeah, probably. And that makes me feel like a total asshole. She shouldn't have to make me worry just to get me to come visit." I covered my eyes with my arm and sighed. "Just sucks that I lost my job, my apartment, my boyfriend, *and* drove the whole way here thinking I was about to lose my grandma, too. Don't get me wrong," I rushed on, "I'm so very glad she's not sick and the Amaryllis seems to be doing well, I just wish she hadn't felt the need to exaggerate to get me here."

"She loves you very much," Vince offered. "She's done nothing but talk about you coming to visit since she heard your plan."

I sat up. "Well, I may feel like a heel for the way she felt she had to get me here, but I'm here now, so I might as well enjoy the time."

Vince sipped his coffee. The man was gorgeous—dark hair, dark eyes, broad shoulders, thighs as thick as logs. I'd never really gone for older men, but the silver streaking through his hair and short stubble seemed to stir something in my gut. The curve of his abdomen under the flannel plaid hinted that his six-pack was well-hidden in the fridge, but even that had my blood warming. Vince was a mountain of a man who looked as if he could break me in two, but he also gave off soft, caring vibes and I suddenly found myself wanting to climb onto his lap and cuddle into his massive frame.

"Sorry to hear about your shitty month," Vince said, his dark eyes studying me over his mug. "That's a lot."

"Yeah," I sighed, pulling myself from fantasies I had no business having over some guy I'd known for an hour. "The job situation sucks, but in reality, it was for the best. I hated the place. The apartment isn't a huge loss, just means I have to find somewhere new once I figure out where I'm going to work."

"And the boyfriend?" A flicker of interest gleamed in Vince's eyes as he waited for my answer.

I shrugged. "He's one of my best friends. He was a friend before we became anything more and he's still a friend." I yawned as the day caught up with me. "We thought adding sex into the mix would be good."

"And it wasn't?"

"I mean, sex is always good—mostly—but it wasn't what we needed from each other. Mike is a great guy and I love him like a brother, but there was no real spark between us. The sex was comfortable, but not the fiery heat of passion movies make you think can happen."

"You don't think it can?" Vince cocked his head.

"I don't know. Never had that with anyone. But sex with Mike was the least passionate. I'm happy for him that he's found someone and we'll always be friends. We went through too much in college to just drift apart." I glanced toward Vince. "What about you? What job did you need to get away from in the city? You have any boyfriend issues to match mine?"

He chuckled. "Well, my boyfriend issue is slightly different and it's mainly the reason I had to leave my job."

"Ohhhh, a scandal?"

"One of my...business associates set me up with her brother." Vince rubbed at his black and silver scruff and I knew he wasn't going to give me specific details about his job. "I wasn't known for long-term relationships, but Cecil and I dated for about six weeks. Things got a bit dicey when he requested I take a look at some of his work. I declined as I never mixed business with pleasure. Come to find out, he'd anonymously submitted work to my place of employment and I'd written a scathing piece about it." Vince scowled. "I don't know that I can say much more, but suffice it to say that my reputation took a bit of a hit and shit hit the fan between Cecil, his sister, and me when everything got out. My ethics were questioned, my firm was pissed, my friend was offended, Cecil was angry and hurt, and I realized I needed a change." He waved his hand. "I had no intention of moving to Holly Hills. Just drove up the hill one day to see what was up here. I left with no intention of returning, but something drew me back and I've been here ever since."

I bit my lip and tried not to grin. "It's the Christmas magic." I nodded sagely.

"Ha, Christmas magic my ass. Come look at this plant Mary Joy swears will thrive with enough Christmas magic." Vince stood and pulled me to my feet.

I stumbled and crashed into his ample chest with a grunt.

Vince caught me and held tight, my arms bent between us, my hands splayed against his chest. For the briefest moment, our eyes met and something passed between us—something hot and needy, like a promise of things to come—and my breath caught in my throat. Telling myself it would be ridiculous to press a kiss against his tantalizing Adam's apple or nuzzle my nose into his inviting scruff, I swallowed thickly.

Vince's gaze lingered for a split-second too long on my lips, his hands unnecessarily gripping the back of my t-shirt, before clearing his throat and taking a step back. "Sorry," he said, his words gruff. "You okay?"

Forgetting the stumble which had put us in that position in the first place, I wondered for a moment why I wouldn't be okay. But then I realized what he was talking about and nodded. "Yeah, all good. Um, so, show me this plant."

Vince led me to the picture window where a large potted Christmas cactus sat in a place of honor right in the middle of a shelving unit. The poor plant had definitely seen better days, but it didn't look completely dead. The flowers were a pretty shade of pinkish red—or they would have been if the plant wasn't on its last leg—and the green, toothed leaves appeared somewhat wilted.

"So, Mary Joy gave me this plant at Thanksgiving. It was gorgeous. She promised it was easy to care for and all I needed to do was place it next to a window with indirect light and water it every two to three weeks." Vince gestured toward the failing plant. "I swear I've done exactly what she told me and just look at it. I've killed plants before, but this may be a record."

"She's really good with plants. If she thinks it will pull through and thrive, I believe her."

Vince scoffed. "She thinks *love and Christmas magic* will save the plant."

I cocked my head as I studied him. "I think she's determined that love and Christmas magic will save you, too." I had no idea why I'd said the words. I had even less idea why something tugged deep in my soul for this man. But suddenly, I was determined to show him what love and Christmas magic could do.

"I don't need saving. I'm happy here," Vince protested.

"Are you? Really?"

He shrugged and averted his eyes. "Yeah, I like it here."

"Do you date much?"

Vince snorted.

I nodded. "That's what I thought. Aren't you lonely?"

"Aren't you?" he shot back.

I took a step closer, wanting more than anything to feel the heat of his big body pressed against mine again and wondering just what the actual fuck I was doing. It was as if I'd been spelled by the magic and was helpless against the attraction between Vince and me. "I mean, I probably have more choices in the city, but yeah, I get lonely."

"So, what's your point?" Vince's gaze dropped to my mouth. "What does love and Christmas magic have to do with two snowed-in strangers forced to share a house?"

I licked my lips, loving the flare of his nostrils and stepped even closer. "Not sure *love* has anything to do with it, and the *magic* may only be in the bedroom, but I have no qualms over a holiday fling if you're down for it."

Vince shook his head. "I already told you, getting involved with a friend's family member got me in trouble once before."

"Not good enough." I spread my hands against his chest and tilted my chin up to meet his eyes. "We have no reason to be involved professionally—hell, I don't even know what *profession* you were in—there's absolutely no conflict of interest."

"You're too young for me," Vince protested, even as his hands settled on my hips.

"We're consenting adults, age has no bearing here." I feathered my lips over his scruffy jawline and delighted in his shuddering groan.

"You're leaving. Long-distance never works." Vince tried once more, but his resolve was dwindling, I could feel his desire pressed against my lower abdomen.

"I'm saying we can have fun while I'm here. I'm not suggesting we continue anything once I leave." A weird zing of something traveled through me as I saw what I thought to be disappointment cross Vince's face.

You don't really have anywhere to go. You could stay for as long as you wanted.

I pushed the thoughts away. I was suggesting a holiday fling, not a long-term relationship with wedding bells. There was a very good chance that Vince and I had absolutely nothing in common and the heat between us would fizzle the moment we stepped out of the bedroom.

He teaches art classes and he's friends with Mary Joy, you've got that going for you already.

I scolded my mind, I wasn't *trying* to have anything in common with Vince. I was *trying* to offer him a body to warm his bed for however long I was in Holly Hills.

"And if we agree to this? What are the parameters?" Vince's eyes bored into mine as his tight fists gripped my hips.

"We have fun, enjoy the time we've got, don't take anything too seriously, and see what happens." I shrugged and bit my lip. "We're likely stuck in this house for at least a week. Hell, by the end of that time, you may be sick of me and ready to throw me in a snow bank. Let's just let things happen." I gave in and pressed a kiss against his neck, loving the groan of pleasure that vibrated against my lips. "Oh, and

I'm going to do everything I can to make you love Christmas."

Vince scoffed. "Not gonna happen, but you can have fun trying."

Rising up on my tiptoes, I nuzzled my nose against his ear. "Challenge accepted," I whispered.

Vince gripped my chin and growled as he lowered his head to devour my mouth.

With a gasp, I opened for his seeking tongue and nearly dropped to my knees as his heat invaded my mouth. We kissed until we needed to breathe and broke apart, panting.

Vince lifted me and carried me back to the pile of blankets. My heart clenched in my tight chest as he gently lowered me and settled himself between my legs—I'd been so right about the gentle giant. With hot, needy kisses pressed against my neck before capturing my lips again, Vince rocked his hips and rubbed our rock-hard cocks together.

"What do you want?" I murmured against his mouth.

"I'm vers and the thought of spreading myself open for you is definitely on my to-do list, but not right now." Vince lifted my chin. "We've got time, don't want to rush anything. What do you want?"

I dropped my hand between us and palmed his dick. "Want this stretching me open at some point. But tonight? I wanna suck you, taste you on my tongue."

Holy fucking shit. How had we gone from chatting with Mary Joy and looking at Vince's almost-dead plant to discussing sexual positions and blow jobs?

Vince rolled over and shucked his clothes off. "Get naked, wanna feel you against me," he demanded.

Still reeling from how quickly we'd moved from idle chit-chat between strangers to flesh-against-flesh and the promise of oral sex, I eagerly obeyed, tossing my clothes to the side.

Vince propped himself on an elbow as he spread out next

to me, his eyes roaming my body as his hand reached out to caress my chest, my belly, the sprinkling of light brown hair leading from my navel to my cock. "You're gorgeous," he murmured.

I brought my hand to his chest and sifted through the thick salt-n-pepper hair covering his skin. "Love this," I said, leaning in to flick a nipple with my tongue before biting gently. "Mmmm, you like that?" I asked when Vince shuddered.

In answer, Vince wrapped an arm around my waist and pulled me close before rolling me to my back and devouring my mouth as his hips slotted between mine and our leaking cocks pressed together.

It had been a very long time since I'd hooked up with someone I barely knew, but this situation didn't feel wrong. In fact, despite the fact I'd known Vince for less than a day, his hands on my body, his lips on me, his cock rutting against my own, it all felt perfectly right. Completely different for me, but right all the same.

Our fevered lust slowed slightly as Vince's tongue explored my mouth, his arms wrapped around me as our hips rocked together. I reached between our bodies and took his thick cock in hand, stroking gently as Vince growled against my lips.

"Wanna taste you," I said, thumbing through the wetness on his slit.

Vince quickly shifted his position, moving both of us to our sides and lining up his mouth with my dick. Faced with his cock bobbing right at eye-level, I licked my lips and took him in my mouth just as Vince trailed his tongue up my throbbing shaft.

"Oh fuck," I panted, my lips feathering over his cock head as he gripped my length and swirled his tongue around my tip.

When Vince took me deep to the back of his throat while fondling my balls, I realized I needed to catch up. I teased my tongue into his slit as I cupped his heavy sac and spread my lips to take his width deep. Loving the silky slide of his hard flesh between my lips, his cock head caressing the roof of my mouth, and his bitter saltiness bursting on my tongue, I bobbed my head and played with his balls, pressing my finger against his taint.

Vince's groan vibrated around my cock before he took me deeper, burying his nose in the short thatch of hair at my base. When he swallowed around my throbbing cock, my balls drew up tight and I ran a hand through his hair, popping off his dick long enough to warn him I was close.

Ignoring my words, Vince fisted his cock and pressed it against my lips. "Suck me, want my cock between your pretty lips when you blow."

His words sent me over the edge and I pulsed my release onto his tongue with a moan just as his cock exploded hot, thick splashes at the back of my throat. Vince gripped my ass and pulled me closer. With a final shudder, I let my dick slip from his mouth as I licked his cock head clean and wiped his release from my lips with the back of my hand.

Shifting so I could be face-to-face with him, I smiled before pressing a kiss against his lips. "Believe in Christmas magic yet?"

Vince chuckled. "No, but there's definitely some kinda magic on your lips. You're fucking amazing." He frowned.

"No, no frowning. That was really good. Let's get cleaned up and fix dinner. Then I'm going to crash because I'm exhausted." I rolled from the pile of blankets and grabbed my clothes. Glancing over my shoulder, I winked and swayed my hips a bit more than necessary as I walked toward the bathroom.

I stared at myself in the mirror. Was it weird that I didn't feel bad about sucking off the guy who'd rescued me in the middle of a snowstorm? It wasn't my norm—I usually needed to know the guy for a while—but I had this easy trust for Vince. Maybe because I knew Mary Joy knew him and loved him—hell, she was very definitely not even trying to hide the fact that she was matchmaking. Maybe it was the crazy intensity between us or the fact that I needed a break from all the bad of the past month. Either way, I didn't feel the least bit guilty.

I wasn't a firm believer in all of the *love and Christmas magic* Mary Joy liked to go on about, but I wasn't one to deny that certain unexplainable things happened in Holly Hills— especially around Christmas time. If that meant bringing some happiness to Vince, I was all for it. Hell, I'd even welcome a little of it coming my way.

Vince wasn't exactly a Grinch, at least from what I could tell, but he seemed to be missing a spark. Maybe this holiday would be just what he needed—maybe it was just what I needed as well.

FOUR

VINCE

I WOKE the next morning and a fresh wave of guilt washed over me.

What in the hell had I done?

Rolling over, I glanced at the angel in my bed. Kota was in the middle of the mattress, his light brown lashes fanned over his pale skin, that gorgeous blond hair a crazy mess of bedhead, and his pretty pink lips parted just slightly as he breathed slowly and steadily in his slumber.

My head wanted me to feel disgusted with the way I'd taken advantage of the kid, but my heart—and my body—insisted there'd been something between us outside of just a carnal lust. I'd met Kota yesterday—for fuck's sake, *yesterday*—and I already knew the weight of his cock on my tongue, the unique scent of his body, the flavor of his release.

Random, nameless, one-night-only hookups were nothing new for me, but what Kota and I had shared was different on so many levels. For one, I *knew* him and counted his grandmother as one of my good friends. For two, we were stuck in the house for several days—I couldn't walk away and never see him again.

And the worst part, the part I couldn't even allow myself to think about because Kota was leaving all-too-soon, was the fact that *nothing* I'd ever had with other men had ever shaken me to the core like what I'd shared with Kota.

I closed my eyes, berating myself as the thought tried to take root in my head. Kota was amazing and I definitely felt some crazy, intense connection to him that I'd never felt with anyone else. But he was leaving. He had no interest in living in Holly Hills. He had a life to get back to. Just because I was lonely didn't mean I had any right to fantasize about what could maybe happen between us.

He offered a holiday fling for as long as he's here.

I pinched the bridge of my nose. If I was smart, I'd refuse the offer. One encounter with Kota had proven enough to burn me alive. It would be for the best if I shut down whatever flamed to life between us and we spent the rest of his time here as just friends.

"You're staring," Kota mumbled as he cracked a sleepy eye.

"Sorry."

"For staring or something else?" He opened both eyes and yawned.

"For taking advantage last night." I swallowed thickly. Right here. I needed to tell him it would never happen again.

"Excuse me?" Kota popped up on his elbow, the sheet slipping to reveal a creamy shoulder. "You didn't force your cock into my mouth and you certainly didn't *make me* slide my dick between your lips."

His words set fire to my blood and I had to grip my raging morning wood in hopes of calming myself down. "I'm just saying that I shouldn't have let things go so far."

Kota cocked his head. "Was it bad? Did you not enjoy it?"

I huffed. "Best sex I ever had." I never should have shared that, but it was the truth.

"Same." Kota reached out and ran a hand down my arm, moving the sheet away as he went, and fit his hand around mine as I palmed my erection. "I'd never ask you to do something you didn't want to do and you can call it quits on this the moment it's no longer good for you. But why not enjoy it while we can? We'll do all things Christmas and burn up the sheets. When it's time for me to leave, we'll have a fun little fling to remember fondly and *you* will hopefully feel at least a little something for Christmas."

Something ached deep inside, tugging at my heart, at the thought of saying goodbye to Kota. But I just nodded. "Okay, as long as you follow the same rules. If it ever gets to a point where it's no longer something you want, just say the word."

Kota grinned and rolled on top of me, straddling my chest as his morning wood bobbed above my face. "I want breakfast, but we've got time for this first. If you're down?"

I groaned and gripped his hips as I opened my mouth. Kota smeared his precum against my bottom lip with a wicked grin. "Suck me off and then I'm going to make you come so hard you see stars." He fed me his cock inch-by-glorious-inch before grabbing the headboard and rocking his hips, his ass pressing against my chest.

Already addicted to the scent and flavor of this man, I groaned around his shaft as it slid between my lips. Moving my hands to his ass, I parted his cheeks and teased a finger against his hole.

Kota's rocking rhythm faltered as he gasped. "Yes, please, I wanna feel you in me."

I put two fingers to his lips and let him suck them, tongue them, and soak them with his spit. After slicking his hole with the wetness, I pressed a finger into him slowly, watching ecstasy fill his face as he continued to thrust his cock into my mouth.

"More, I want more," Kota begged as I fucked his ass with one finger.

Loving the way he begged, I worked a second finger into him, breaching his tight muscle as he gasped and increased his rhythm.

"Shit, Vince, I'm gonna come," Kota warned as his hips rocked and I finger-fucked him. He gripped the headboard and fucked into me, once, twice, three times before moaning and shooting his load onto my tongue as his ass clenched around my fingers. My cock twitched at the thought of being buried in his perfect ass as he came.

Kota took a moment to catch his breath as I slid my fingers from his body. Then he shifted from my chest and knee-walked to between my legs. "Scoot up some, if you wanna watch."

I moved to prop myself against the headboard and hissed when he buried his head between my thighs and lifted my balls so he could press his hot, wet tongue against my taint. With one hand, he stroked my cock, with the other hand he slicked a finger in his mouth and teased it against my hole.

A familiar, welcome sting washed over me as he slipped his finger into me and I thrust my hips, praying he'd suck me soon. Kota seemed to know what I was thinking because he grinned and shifted to a position that allowed him to work his pretty pink lips around my thick shaft while still sliding his finger in and out of my ass.

I groaned when he added a second finger and his moan vibrated around my throbbing cock. "Fuck, Kota, so damn good. Fuck. Gonna come."

If I'd thought I could possibly hold off for a bit, all hope of that flew out the window when he crooked his fingers and brushed over the bundle of nerves deep inside. I nearly came off the bed as my release exploded, shooting hot and thick onto Kota's tongue.

Removing his fingers from my ass and allowing my spent dick to slip from between his lips, Kota shimmied up my body and pressed a messy, wet kiss against my mouth. We smelled of sweat and sex, his tongue tasted of me and mine of him, and it was a wake-up I never wanted to forget.

"Good morning," Kota whispered against my lips. "Guess what we're going to do today."

I groaned and gripped the back of his head, deepening the kiss, savoring our mixed flavors.

When we finally broke apart, Kota smiled. "Mmmm, yes, we can do more of that. But later."

Gripping his perfect ass, I cocked a brow. "Just what are you up to?"

"We're going to get a tree and decorate for Christmas. Full-on day of decorating. Cut down the tree, Christmas music, cookies baking, a cheesy holiday movie on TV, a fire blazing."

I groaned. "Noooo."

"Yes. But showers and breakfast first. I'm thinking pancakes? Have you ever made Mary Joy's buttermilk pancakes?" Kota tweaked my nipples and pressed one final kiss to my lips before he stood and cocked a hand on his hip.

"Has anyone ever told you you're gorgeous?" Seriously, he was so damn perfect with those icy-blue eyes, messy blond hair, long, lean body, and sexy-as-sin smile. I stood and faced him, staring down at his beautiful body.

Kota poked a finger against my chest. "I'll take the compliment, and you're beyond fucking gorgeous, but I'm not going to be distracted. We're doing this."

"Fine. Let's get started. I'll help with the pancakes, but I've only ever eaten them, never made them."

Kota smiled and threw his arms around my neck. "Pancakes, a whole day of Christmas fun, and then tonight, I have other plans."

I cocked a brow. "What other plans?"

He pressed his already-hard-again cock against my thigh —damn youthful recovery time—and licked my nipple. "If you're a good boy, maybe you'll find out."

Thirty-minutes later, we were in the kitchen with Christmas tunes playing while Kota danced around gathering ingredients.

"Good thing we're stocked for the storm. The thought of being snowed-in isn't as bad when you know you're not going to starve." Kota dumped an armful of supplies on the kitchen island. "If we haven't lost power yet, you think we're going to?"

I shook my head. "I'm thinking we're mostly past that worry. The snow has already tapered off a little. Even if it goes down, we've got a back-up generator, so we should be good." Rolling up the sleeves of my sweatshirt, I joined Kota at the counter. "Tell me what to do."

"Have you made pancakes before?"

I rolled my eyes. "Yes."

He grinned. "Okay, okay, just checking. So, we're going to get this all mixed up and then you can man the griddle while I work on the bacon."

I'd never in my life cooked with a man after sex. Hell, I'd never in my life cooked with a man, period. Kota and I fell into an easy rhythm and I found myself humming along to the stupid Christmas songs as he sang.

When I poured the first pancake, the griddle sizzled and my humming continued. Kota slid a baking sheet of bacon into the hot oven before wrapping his arms around me, pressing his front to my side while he kissed my shoulder. "Careful," he whispered, "you're looking a little too jolly for someone who hates Christmas."

I huffed and poured more pancakes. "It's not that I *hate* Christmas."

"You just don't believe in love and Christmas magic?"

"I've never been in love. The job I used to have made it so I never knew if the guys I hooked up with wanted more with me because of *me* or because of my name. Nothing ever clicked between us and I accepted a long time ago that love just isn't something I'm cut out for." I watched the pancakes bubble around the edges and flipped one.

"Just because it's not happened yet, doesn't mean it won't happen." Kota ran a hand up and down my back.

"Pretty sure there's a statute of limitations and at my age…"

"Shut. Up." Kota slapped my ass. "You're forty-four, not ninety-four. Good God, man, don't talk like you're ancient. Love has no time restrictions or age limits."

I shrugged and flipped the last pancake. "I just don't know if it's for me. Plus, if I've never been in love, how would I even know if it's something I want?"

Kota shook his head. "I can't say for sure. I've *thought* I was in love a couple times before, but maybe I wasn't. I think maybe it's one of those things that kinda punches you right in the face and when you know, you know. Plus, I don't think love cares if it's something *you want*, love just happens."

"Do you believe in Mary Joy's Christmas magic?" I asked, stacking pancakes onto a plate before pouring new batter onto the griddle and enjoying the satisfying sizzle.

"Not the way she does, but yeah, I do."

"How? Aren't you some graphic design prodigy? That doesn't really sound like a profession that believes in magic." I spread butter on the stack of waiting pancakes.

"I'm not a prodigy," Kota scoffed. "I love graphic design, but I also love all kinds of art. I think that's one of the reasons I was so unhappy at my job. They had certain boxes and templates and requirements; I wasn't allowed to really unleash my creative side. I want to work in a way that doesn't feel like work, share my art with others, be open to really *create*." He shrugged. "But that's neither here nor there." He waved a hand before checking the bacon. "I can't say for sure about the magic. I just know there's something special about this place and it's even more evident at Christmas."

"Like what? I need examples."

Kota grinned. "That's just it, I can't say for sure any hard-and-fast examples. But I know there's this *feeling*. And my entire life, I've heard of Christmas magic coming through for jobs, healing, money for gifts, a loved one coming home, a new tire showing up to replace a flat, shoes for an interview appearing out of nowhere, a check for exactly the amount of rent being stuffed in a mailbox, those sorts of things."

I turned the pancakes. "My parents would say that's God's work. In fact, they'd probably damn you to hell for claiming *magic*."

Kota shrugged. "Well, for one, I don't like your parents very much. Sorry, not sorry. Two, many would claim Christmas magic is very much God's work. What's it matter what we call it? I'm not a super religious person—and many of *God's people* are the reason I've been turned off organized religion—but I can't deny there are good things that happen. Whether that's God or Christmas magic or something else or a combination, I don't know. I don't *count* on it. I don't think it's the only way to get answers or good news or whatever. But I do know that I love the way I feel when I'm here and I've seen bits and pieces of that magic in my lifetime. Mary Joy believes more because she's been around to see it for a lot longer than me."

I piled more pancakes onto the plate. "Maybe you just feel good here because you're with family and good folks, eating good food, celebrating a holiday you've always loved."

Kota pulled the bacon from the oven before turning to

look at me. "Maybe. But I like to think it's the Christmas magic all the same. It's kinda fun to believe in it. Plus, love and magic aside, I love all that goes into Christmas. Don't get me wrong, I *don't* love the crowds and rude people and greedy consumerism and all of that. But what we're going to do today? Being outside and finding our perfect tree? Decorating the house? Baking and watching cheesy movies? All of that brings back my childhood and I adore it."

His words lit something in me. If Kota loved this time of year so much, I'd do my best to make sure he got the Christmas he came here for. Even if *I* wasn't as into it, I could pretend to be for Kota's sake. Fake it 'til you make it, right?

"Well, I have only terrible memories of decorating for Christmas, so you'll have to teach me all the good things about it." I turned off the griddle.

"I'm on it, but let's eat first." Kota carried a plate of bacon to the table and I followed with two plates of pancakes.

After settling in and getting my stack doused in real maple syrup—none of that fake crap for Mary Joy—I took a bite and groaned. "Oh my God, these are amazing."

"Right?" Kota grinned around a bite. "It's the buttermilk. I don't like the big, fluffy, cakey pancakes, I want these thin ones. Soooo, good."

We ate in comfortable silence for a moment before Kota spoke again.

"I didn't know how lonely I was feeling with Mike gone and my roommates moving out." He stared at his plate. "I know this is short-term and not a real answer to anything— and it's *crazy* how easy and comfortable this feels—but it's nice and I think it's something I really needed." He shrugged, his cheeks pinking. "So, you know, thanks...for being my holiday fling." Kota flashed me a flirty smile.

I chuckled. "Yeah, I get it. This may be the forced holiday intervention I never would have admitted I needed."

Kota smiled and went back to eating.

I shoved a bite of delicious pancake in my mouth and followed it quickly with crispy bacon in hopes of staving off the ridiculous thoughts I was having. Thoughts like how comfortable it was to be sharing breakfast with Kota. How easy he was to talk to. How warm and relaxed I was while spending time with him.

And how soon our little holiday fling would be just a distant memory.

Maybe he doesn't have to leave. He's out of a job. Maybe he could get something remote and work from Holly Hills.

I washed down my breakfast and the insane notion with a swig of coffee. No, Kota had made it clear he came here to visit Mary Joy, maybe help out a bit, and then he'd be back to his real life.

After loading the dishwasher and cleaning up the kitchen, we went to the hall closet where all of the winter gear was kept.

"I've got a coat, but snow pants and boots would be good," Kota said as he browsed through the items available.

"Well, I've always teased Mary Joy that she's got enough in here to fill a sporting goods store, so I'm sure there are things that will fit." I tossed him a hat. "Don't forget gloves."

Kota stuck the hat on his head. "Oh, we'll need the ax. Or maybe a saw?" Then he glanced my way. "So, in theory, cutting down our own tree sounds great. In reality, I've never actually cut down a tree."

My eyes went wide and I couldn't help but laugh. "Mr. Holly Jolly Christmas Boy? How can that be?"

Kota huffed and rolled his eyes. "First, I'm not *that* bad about Christmas. In fact, on the way here, I was lamenting the fact that I was going to be stuck in Holly Jolly Christmas Town hell surrounded by happy, joyful people."

I cocked a brow. "And now?" I was fishing, but I didn't even care.

He shrugged. "Now, it doesn't seem so bad." He held up two fingers. "Second, we always had real trees, but we got them at a tree lot most of the time. The few times we went out to cut one down, I was too little to use the saw or ax."

I rubbed my hands together. "Well then, I guess we'll learn together."

Thirty minutes later, we were dressed in several layers as we headed out the door.

"I think it's best to head to the back of the property," I told Kota. "There's a bigger selection of trees and we don't have to worry about cutting down something Mary Joy wants to keep."

"Good idea," Kota said as we started toward the tree line. "Damn, this is deep." The snow was over our knees in many places. "My legs will be sore tomorrow."

I shot him a look, not sure if he could see my smirk.

"From walking through the snow and, *perhaps*, other things," he teased. He paused and glanced around. "Look at this. There's no way you can see this beautiful scene and *not* feel just a little bit magical."

"It's gorgeous," I said, staring at Kota for a split second too long before gazing around at the calm, quiet sea of snow. Once the storm moved on and the sun came out, we'd be surrounded by a blinding field of icy sparkles. "Definitely feeling *something*."

Kota caught my eye and a look—deep, meaningful, full of promise—passed between us. Or maybe that was just my wishful heart.

What was it about this man? I'd been doing just fine on my own, minding my business and building some semblance of a happy, content life in Holly Hills. And then Kota Scott showed up and tipped my world on its axis. He had me wanting and wishing for things I'd never had, things I didn't even know I wanted until he came to town.

Things I couldn't have because he was leaving after the holiday season.

"So, you said you only have terrible memories of Christmas. Tell me about them," Kota said.

I shook my head as we continued our trek. "No, I said I had only terrible memories of *decorating* for Christmas. I actually used to love the holiday. As a young child, I loved the gifts, the special songs at church, waking up early, the baked goods, having family over. I didn't come out until a little before I turned sixteen, but I think my parents suspected. The preaching, demeaning comments, and damning me to hell started even before I admitted I was gay. I think it all started when I was about ten, that's when I first remember my parents talking about the sins of homosexuals a lot. They didn't ever say anything directly about me, but they made sure I heard—which made it all the harder to finally accept myself and tell them about my true self. Honestly, if it wasn't for my aunt, I'm not sure how I would have survived the rest of my teen years with them. Pretty sure they would have shipped me off to some sort of conversion camp." I blinked away the memory like a snowflake on my lashes. "But the nightmare of decorating for Christmas started long before that."

Kota touched my arm. I barely felt it through the thick layers, but the gesture meant something all the same.

"My parents couldn't do anything without fighting. House projects, washing the car, going grocery shopping, decorating for Christmas, everything ended in a huge fight. One of the first Christmases I remember was filled with broken lights and ornaments. One of the last ones involved a tree being tossed out the front door." I shook my head at the memory. "Don't get me wrong, by the time family or friends showed up, the veil was back in place and everything appeared to be holly, jolly perfect and blessed by God. But leading up to that point was always a nightmare and I hated it."

"Damn, it's no wonder you're not super crazy about Christmas." Kota paused as we reached the edge of the wooded area. "Maybe we can make some good memories to replace the shitty ones."

"I'm down for that," I said and lifted the saw in my hand. "Let's get a tree, I'm freezing."

"Yep, hot chocolate is in store when we get back."

"Make mine coffee and you've got yourself a deal."

Kota took off through the woods. "It's not as deep in here," he said. "Listen. It's so quiet."

We stood in the middle of the wooded area, surrounded by deafening silence. The snow had fallen through the trees, but a lot of it was on the branches and hadn't reached the ground. How a scene could be so perfectly calm and quiet— breathtakingly beautiful—I'd never know, but I was grateful I'd ended up in that place and that moment.

A shiver shook me from my reverie and I motioned toward a small tree at the edge of the woods. "How big are you wanting it?"

Kota turned mischievous eyes my way. "Oh, I'm not too much of a size queen. I think it's more about knowing what to do with it, ya know?" He bit his lip, trying not to grin.

"Noted." I winked. "If the *tree* is going to be in the living room, it can be a bit taller and fuller than that one. If we want it elsewhere, it probably needs to be about that size."

Kota walked toward the small tree. "This one is so cute, but I think I want it bigger and fuller." Again, he cast a flirty glance my way.

"I'll give you bigger and fuller," I growled as I gripped his coat and pulled him in for a kiss.

It was too icy cold for the kiss to set fire to anything, but the press of our lips sealed a promise of what was to come.

"The tree, I was just talking about the tree," Kota said innocently.

"Mmhm." I pointed the saw toward a group of trees farther down. "All of these tall trees are deciduous, but it seems like quite a few evergreens surround the wooded area. I'm guessing they're much younger than these big hardwood trees."

"Ohhhh." Kota's word hung in like a cloud in the icy air as we reached the trees in question. "This one looks good. No holes on this side." He walked around the back. "Only one bare spot back here and it can go in the corner. What do you think? Perfection?"

As far as Christmas trees went, it really was a good-looking specimen. "It's like the tree grew right here just for us," I teased, but I was more serious than joking. Everything from the moment I spotted Kota's car seemed as if it had been perfectly planned—mapped out just for us—and I wasn't really sure what to do with that.

"Right?" Kota's icy blue eyes sparkled. "This beauty has been growing for years, just waiting for the winter that a gorgeous Grinch and a homeless grandson find their way to Holly Hills and set forth to make the most of their snowed-in holiday." He pretended to hug the tree. "We're here, Beauty, you don't have to wait any longer."

I chuckled. "Yeah, we're here. Now we're going to hack you off at the base and drag you to your eventual death."

Kota gasped. "Shhh, not in front of the child." He mimed covering the tree's ears. "She will stand in a place of honor and glory, bringing her beauty and much enjoyment to all who see her." He winced. "Before she eventually dies a slow, thirsty, dry death. Oh, shit, now I feel bad."

I cocked a brow. "It's up to you. Cut her down or go treeless?"

Kota glanced around. "She's so pretty. I say we take her and make her last moments glorious—you never know who else might come looking for a tree and treat her poorly in her final days."

I couldn't help but smile. "You've got quite the imagination there." I reached into the tree and took hold of the trunk, giving it a good, hard shake to get the snow off the branches. "Okay, I need you to hold it while I work on the base."

"Mmm," Kota teased, "sounds kinky."

"Damn, you're that person, huh?"

Kota frowned. "What person?"

"The person who can turn almost anything into something sexual."

He smiled broadly. "Yes. Yes, I am."

I waited until he reached deep into the tree to grip the trunk and then I got on the ground and shimmied under the lowest branches. "How is it that I ended up being the one on the cold ground cutting down a tree when it's *you* insisting we get a tree?"

"You're a gentleman, showing chivalry at its finest," Kota said from above as I began to saw. "Plus, you know that I'm too soft-hearted to actually cut into her. It's almost as if I can hear the sounds of her weeping even now."

I chuckled and continued to work the saw back and forth. The tree really was gorgeous, but it wasn't terribly big. Luckily for us since I wasn't sure the little hand saw could have made it through a thick trunk. "I'm about halfway through. Trying to keep the base even for when we put it in the stand," I explained. "Guess we can even it up back at the house if needed. Be ready to hold it up."

In the next few minutes, I freed the tree from its base and

Kota laid it gently to its side while I stood and brushed snow and dirt from my clothes. "Pretty sure these gloves are ruined. So much sap."

Kota laughed. "It's like that old movie. The one where the guy is all about Christmas and he knocks the whole town out of power when he finally gets his lights working?"

"Christmas Vacation?" I asked.

"Yeah, remember the scene when they go get a tree from the woods and he ends up covered in sap? Everything is sticking to him, the magazine pages, his wife's hair." He laughed again. "I love that movie."

"It's a classic," I agreed. "I don't really do a lot of re-watching movies, but that's one I'll watch over and over. I think I kinda relate to a lot of it. The annoying chaos, the let-down of the lights and the meal, the unwanted family members showing up, the disappointment...I know it's just a comedy and overall it turns out to be a great holiday for them, but the negatives always stick out to me as the most realistic." I frowned. "I'm kinda surprised you've seen that one. Most kids your age don't seem to appreciate the older movies."

"First," Kota cocked a hip, "I'm not a kid. We've been over this several times. Full-grown man here—I've got the...well, I was going to say job and apartment to prove it, but that's clearly not the case at this exact moment. I've got my ID back at the house if you need proof I'm a man."

Stepping away from the tree, I wrapped my arms around him—a feat with both of us wearing so many layers—and tipped up his chin before kissing him, sweeping my tongue into his warm mouth. "No proof needed, last night and this morning was more than enough evidence. Sorry, I know you're grown, I just feel old."

Kota nodded and returned to the kiss until breaking away with a smirk. "Second, I love old movies. Mary Joy and I used to watch them. I don't like the *really* old holiday classics as much as the ones that are more your generation."

"Oh my God, I just told you I feel old and you go right for the jugular with your very next words. Low blow, man." I held a hand to my chest.

"What?" Kota batted his lashes. "I'm just saying that Christmas Vacation was probably made when you were born, right? It might even be older than you."

"I doubt that. But there's no need to further my pain. In fact, my *old* knees are likely about to seize up, better get your elder back to the house."

Kota laughed. "I'll look it up once I have my phone. I wasn't calling you *old*, I was simply saying I prefer movies of your generation over movies of Mary Joy's generation."

"You should stop talking now," I deadpanned.

We hefted the tree up and made our way back to the house.

Once on the porch, we gave the tree another good shaking and then brought it through the door.

"I'll get the tree stand. You make sure the base is flat." Kota stripped out of his winter gear in the small utility room. "We should let all of this hang out here to dry. Once we get the tree in the stand, let's clean up and get something warm to drink. I'm thinking we get some cookies baking and then we'll start the decorating."

"Perfect. And if a nap is available in the day's plans, even better. Gotta remember, I'm old." I spread my wet jacket over the bench.

"Oh my God, you're not old. I'll prove it tonight when we go at least two rounds."

"Now *that* would be Christmas magic," I teased.

FIVE
KOTA

"HEY," I hollered as I walked through the living room, phone in hand after we'd settled the tree in its stand and moved it to a corner wall. "What year were you born?"

Vince popped his head around the corner. "1977. Why?"

"Oh," I squeaked. "Never mind."

"Kota," he drew my name out threateningly. "Why?"

I grimaced. "I was wrong about the movie date, no biggie."

Vince walked over to where I was standing in front of the large picture window and grabbed my phone. He scanned it quickly and then huffed out a humorless laugh. "So, the *classic* of *my generation* that you love so much came out in 1989." He pursed his lips. "So, basically what you've just proven to me is that I'm older than your favorite *classic*. Does that make me ancient? Prehistoric?"

I yanked my phone away from him and wrapped my arms around him, tipping my head up for a kiss. I knew the moment Vince was no longer worried about his age or the stupid movie because heat filled his eyes as his mouth dropped to mine. His lips were firm and demanding, but there was a soft protectiveness to his kiss—as if he wanted to own me and keep me safe all at once—and I couldn't help the whimper that escaped me.

Vince turned us so my ass was against the shelving unit and I spread my legs for him. We'd both changed into sweats and I suddenly wanted to forget all about decorating and baking—my mind had one track and it led to bed with Vince's cock buried in my ass. Something on the second shelf toppled over and my thigh bumped into a solid object to my left. "Oh shit, careful of the plant," I murmured against Vince's mouth. "Mary Joy would have both our asses if we killed her plant in a blaze of horniness."

Vince pulled me close and kissed me hard and deep before breaking away. "It's almost dead anyway, but yeah, probably shouldn't knock it to its death."

I glanced down at the Christmas cactus and frowned. "Damn, did you give it Miracle-Gro or something?"

Vince picked up a few odds and ends we'd knocked over in our haste to tongue-fuck each other's mouths before he turned to the plant. "No, why? Oh." He peered down at the plant. "That's weird. It looks less dead, right?"

"Yeah, I mean, it still looks sickly and like it *could* die at any moment, but it has a bit more life in it than last night. Did you do anything with it after we looked at it?"

He shook his head. "Not a single thing. Maybe it just liked the attention," he teased. "Maybe it saw how upset I was about it dying and decided to give it one last go."

I raised a brow. "Maybe it's the Christmas magic."

"How did I *know* you were going to say that?" Vince ran a finger over one of the leaves. "Well, whatever it is, let's hope it continues. I really don't want to kill it. Plus, Mary Joy said it's super easy to take care of and I kinda like having it here. Just wish it didn't look so bad."

"We'll keep an eye on it. Maybe it's horny—ohhh, it perked up after what we did out here last night. Maybe we should get kinky in front of it daily and see if that brings it back to life."

Vince stared at me for a moment, blinking slowly as if he wasn't quite sure what to make of me. "I'm not getting kinky for a plant. That's just weird. Like it can watch us? Like it gets turned on and grows because we're having sex?" He shook his head with a chuckle. "No, just no."

I shrugged. "The other option is to believe it's Christmas magic. Your choice."

Vince reached for me with a growl, but I yelped and ran toward the kitchen.

"Come on, it's time for hot chocolate and cookie baking," I told him as I set the water to boil. "Which kinds do you want to make?"

Vince scowled a bit as he considered the question. "I've never actually baked cookies."

"What?!"

He shrugged. "I lived in the city. It was just as easy to get something delicious from a bakery."

"That's like sacrilege or something. Everyone should bake cookies at least once in their life. What kind are your favorite?"

"I love sugar cookies with icing. Oh, one place used to make these snowball cookies—like a buttery shortbread ball covered in powdered sugar. They melted in your mouth. And snickerdoodles."

"Perfect, I know for a fact that Mary Joy has recipes for all of those. You get the drinks made and turn on a movie while I get the recipes and ingredients."

I pulled out one of Mary Joy's recipe boxes—she'd had all of her recipes duplicated a few years back, plus she barely needed a recipe to cook because she had most of them memorized—and shuffled through the cards to find the three cookies Vince wanted to make.

Vince put two mugs on the island and went to the far counter to turn on the small flat-screen TV my grandma had installed so she could watch or listen while she cooked. Although, she'd pretty much lived at the Amaryllis Inn most of my life, so the TV was likely more for her guests. She'd always hinted that I could move to Holly Hills and live in the guesthouse, maybe she was stocking it with items that would draw me in.

As I watched Vince scan the channels, the warm scent of chocolate and coffee filling the air, I had a brief flash of longing. Would it *really* be that bad to live in Holly Hills? I scoffed and shook my head. First, I couldn't just invite myself to move in with Vince and I'd never ask him to move. Second, I didn't have a job here—nor would there likely *be* any type of job for me here.

With a pang of disappointment, I shook off the ridiculous thought and sorted ingredients.

"Hey, you wanna just do music? I don't know that I can watch anything while focusing on baking." Vince gestured toward the television.

"Sounds good. Turn it on that channel that has the fireplace and music."

"*Any* music?" Vince waggled a brow.

"*Christmas* music, of course." I pretended to flip long hair over my shoulder. "You can't spend a holiday season in a perpetual Christmas town and not listen to sounds-of-the-season-music while baking. It's just not done."

Vince rolled his eyes, but smiled and found the right channel. "The whole perpetual Christmas town is something I was really worried about when I first came here. I had this thought that it would be like that movie Groundhog Day—every single day the same, day in and day out, but with

Christmas." He washed his hands. "But it's not *as* bad as I was imagining. Don't get me wrong, the townsfolk definitely put a bit of Christmas spin on pretty much anything and everything they can get their hands on, but the place is nice and comfortable, people are friendly, and it's a far cry from the pretentious chaos I dealt with in my past. I definitely didn't realize I needed a place like this—would have laughed in the face of anyone who even suggested it—but it's been a welcome reprieve."

I plated several sticks of butter in hopes they'd get to room temperature quickly. "Two questions. First, are you ever going to tell me what you used to do in the city?"

"It's not really all that important. I still dabble in the field a bit, but I'm happy here doing odds and ends and teaching art classes after school." Vince shrugged. "Next question."

I pursed my lips. I had to respect that he didn't want to talk more about his past, but I was so intrigued at what he might have done in his former career. "Fine, but I'm not giving up. Second question, what were your initial thoughts when you came here? I mean, as if Amaryllis Inn isn't bad enough. Did you eat at the Mistletoe on Main diner or shop at Ivy's Grocery *before* deciding this was the place for you? If the Juniper Java Shop and Bakery wasn't what sold you, was it Holly Hills Elementary and Middle School or Winterberry High School?" I cocked a brow. "I don't know, for someone who supposedly hates Christmas, you voluntarily moved to Holiday Hell."

Vince chuckled. "Honestly, I came up here one day just to look around. My plan was to leave the city and drive until I got bored. I'd passed this place on the way west, but on the return trip I decided to venture up the hill. I laughed and rolled my eyes when I saw all the Christmas-themed names, but I had a relaxing afternoon roaming the town and chatting with people. Mary Joy demanded I eat at the Amaryllis for dinner since I'd had breakfast at Juniper Java and lunch at Mistletoe on Main. She convinced me to spend the night at the bed-and-breakfast. When I left the next morning, I'd never felt so relaxed and welcomed. I went on my way, but couldn't shake the feeling of wanting to be here. So, I came back a few weeks later and asked Mary Joy about jobs and places to stay. The rest is history."

I nodded. "I get it. This place has that effect on people. Like, when I'm here, all I want to do is stay. Which isn't possible for me, obviously, but it draws you in and you just feel better being here." I took a sip of my hot chocolate and watched as Vince savored his coffee.

Vince cocked his head as he placed his mug on the counter. "You're in graphic design, yeah?"

"Mmhm. Or, I was. Who knows if I can get another job in the field."

"What made you opt for that?"

I shrugged. "I love art of all kinds. Love being able to create things from a shard of an idea. I thought a degree in graphic design would pay the rent better than attempting to make a living as an artist—I love my art, but *starving artist* didn't seem like the career I wanted to dive into at the time. I love taking my own thoughts and visions—or those of others —and building exactly the right design. Whether it's for a business sign, a magazine layout, a book cover, whatever."

Vince watched me for a moment. "But you *truly* love losing yourself in your art. You enjoy bringing ideas to life in a design, but your heart is in...what kind of art do you do?"

My heart caught. How did this man get me so deeply after such a short amount of time? Swallowing thickly, I smiled as my cheeks heated. "I love to draw. Paper and pencil, pastels, charcoals, markers, even digital drawing."

"And do you have certain subjects you prefer to draw?"

"I can draw pretty much anything. If I can see it or even

just picture it in my head, I can probably bring it to life on paper. I probably struggle the most with the human form, it's definitely not my forte. I love putting animals and nature on paper—I go back and forth between realistic, cartoonish, and abstract, depending on my mood."

Vince stepped close and cupped my cheek. "You absolutely come alive when you talk about your art. Don't ever lose that. Maybe a big advertising firm as a graphic designer isn't your thing, and that's okay. Cling to your passion and never let it go. Don't fixate on needing to be in the city for the perfect job. Your skills, your talent, they're all right here," he brushed fingers over my temple, "you can work from anywhere."

Tears stung my eyes as my heart swelled. "How do you know I'm talented?" And why did hearing words from this man I'd just met mean so much to me?

"I'd love to see your work as proof, but I can feel it when you talk about it."

"I'd love to have a job that paid the rent and allowed me to work from anywhere, but I don't know how to make that happen." I shrugged.

"What's your dream job?"

I took a deep breath. I'd never spoken it aloud before because it seemed small and unrealistic. "I'd love to work independently and provide commissions and contract work for greeting card companies, boutique and small business advertising, possibly specific displays in museums, and niche stores with the right customers for my work." I shrugged, my cheeks warm. "I know it's small and kinda vague, but it's always felt like if I got my work seen by the right people, I could make a living off of it."

"Don't ever think of your dreams as small—the tiniest dreams can lead to big things." Vince leaned in and kissed me, slow and gentle. "After cookies, I'd love to see your work."

"I'll ask Mary Joy if she still has any of my pieces." I recalled the Christmas before when I'd had to cancel. "Oh, last year, she wanted me to create some pieces for the inn and she stocked up on all the supplies I'd need. I'd guess she's still got everything."

"While you're here, if she's okay with it, you should do some pieces and let her sell them. It may not rake in big bucks, but if you provide your contact information, you may get some repeat customers. People are always looking for unique new art. From the casual purchaser who just loves a certain piece to the more serious collector, there are people out there who will devour art of all types. You're right, it's about finding the right audience."

I stared at Vince in wonderment—was he just being a good cheerleader or did he know art?—for a moment before breaking into a soft smile. "Thank you. I think you may have just given me the encouragement I needed to take a step toward making my dream come true. I know it won't happen overnight, but thank you for the boost."

"Always." He rubbed his hands together. "Okay, where do we start?" Vince seemed a little leery, almost as if he'd just given me more information than he meant to.

I tucked that tidbit away for later and grabbed a recipe card.

We spent the next couple hours measuring, sifting, scooping, and waiting. We did the sugar cookies first so they could cool while we worked on the snowballs and snickerdoodles.

"Okay, I think these are ready for the icing," I said when the snowballs were all powdered and the sugar cookies were cool. "Do you want to do fancy or just smear the icing on?"

"Honestly, I'm so ready for a nap, let's just smear it on. It all tastes the same and we aren't entering any contests." Vince yawned. "Is dreaming of a comfy, cozy nap in front of the fire part of Christmas magic? If so, it's hit me hard."

"Do my ears deceive me? Did Vince Carter just possibly suggest he *might* be under the influence of Christmas magic?" I mixed up the buttercream icing and separated it into three bowls—we'd have white, red, and green.

Vince chuckled. "It's the exhaustion talking. I don't think I realized how tiring traipsing all the way to the woods in over a foot of snow would be."

We set to work icing the three dozen sugar cookies, humming to the Christmas songs filling the air, and chatting about random nothingness.

"Want lunch and a movie before we drift off?" I asked as I took a bite of one of the soft, chewy, sugary confections.

"Yes, please. I think I've eaten a pound of sugar during our foray into baking and I need real food." Vince stood behind me as we both peered into the fridge. "Sandwiches? I'm not starving and they'd be easy."

A sound chimed from the living room. "Is that the iPad?"

Vince rushed to get it and I heard him saying hello before Mary Joy's voice filled the house. He came around the corner holding the iPad and smiling as Mary Joy gushed about the two of us making cookies.

"Such good boys, I love seeing you settling in and making the best of being stuck indoors. Once the snow clears a bit, be sure to get into town and see the sights," Grandma continued. "I know folks will just be tickled pink to see you this year, Kota. You really don't know how much they adore having you here in town. Have you given any thought to moving here permanently? Would that boyfriend of yours be willing?"

I had to laugh that she was matchmaking in the midst of trying to persuade me and my boyfriend to move to town. I cleared my throat. "Mike and I are just friends, the dating didn't really work out."

"Oh really," Mary Joy drawled. "Well, it's probably for the best."

I did my best not to glance toward Vince. Did he realize she was trying to set us up? Would he be frustrated with her? Me? Was she wasting her time with the matchmaking? To be honest, it kinda seemed like Vince and I had slotted ourselves together pretty easily without Grandma's meddling.

"All the more reason for you to quit that job of yours and move to Holly Hills. I understand that a lot of jobs these days can be worked from just about anywhere. Maybe you wouldn't even have to quit; the internet up here is great—I swear it's the Christmas magic—maybe your company would let you work remotely. I think it's become all the rage lately." Mary Joy rambled on while pots and pans clanged in the background.

"Well, the job didn't really work out," I said, embarrassed to admit I'd lost the boyfriend, job, and apartment pretty much in one fell swoop. "And my roommates opted for other places now that our lease was up, so I moved out of our place."

Mary Joy leaned in, peering closely at the screen. "Kota Christopher, are you telling me you're completely unattached, looking for a place to live, and in need of a job?"

I winced. "Yes?"

"Well, that settles it. You'll stay here for the time being. I'm not saying you have to settle down permanently, but rent-free living isn't something you can turn down while you're looking for your next place to land."

"I can't..." My eyes darted to Vince.

He shook his head. "Sounds like a good idea, Mary Joy. Plenty of room here. When the inn isn't full, I can take a room there for a while."

"No," my grandmother and I both snapped.

Blushing, I went on. "I just mean, I wouldn't expect to push you out of your house."

"Stuff and nonsense. There's room at the guesthouse for two people." Mary Joy clasped her hands to her chest. "This is such a holiday dream come true. I have my grandson home with me for Christmas. Now, don't expect to just be a couch potato, I need your help once this snow clears."

I nodded, wondering how in the hell I'd just agreed to live with Vince and stay at Holly Hills for the foreseeable future. "No worries, I've got some job-related things to do, but I want to keep busy. I need to know I'm pulling my weight around here if I'm going to be living rent-free."

"Vince, do you think you can get the two of you over here to the inn tomorrow? I've got things that need doing."

Vince smiled and gave me a wink. "Pretty sure we can get there. I think Kota will hold me captive here until the tree is decorated, but we can be over after that."

"Tree?" Mary Joy asked.

"We went out and got a tree this morning," I said. "Vince isn't the most holiday-cheer-filled person and I'm determined to convince him that Christmas isn't all that bad." I elbowed him and winked.

Mary Joy beamed. "I love it. Good luck. I've been trying for two years." She cocked her head. "Maybe he has more reason to believe it coming from you," she murmured.

My cheeks burned and I was grateful when something dinged in the background on Mary Joy's end and she announced it was time to go.

"Oh, Kota, I've got all of your art supplies here—the ones I bought last year? Will you work on some pieces for my guests? I think there are several who would be happy to buy and probably even order more. There's a color printer in the office and I think I have some blank business cards left over from a few years ago. See if you can create something with your contact information so my guests can get ahold of you for future orders." She clucked her tongue. "Honestly, you really should have a website."

"I'll see what I can do," I promised and hung up.

"You know, she's right," Vince said. "Let's eat, nap, and then we can work on the website and business cards. Pretty sure, between the two of us, we can get a good start."

"I don't want to tell her of my plans just yet," I said as we set about making sandwiches and grabbing chips. "If she knows what I'm wanting to do, she'll get it in her head that I'll stay." I held up a hand. "I'm not saying I can't or won't stay, but I have to be realistic. There's not a lot for me to do here and getting my work in front of the right people in order to actually start making a living is a long shot." I shrugged and bit into my sandwich. After chewing and swallowing, I continued. "Just don't want her to get her hopes up and then be upset when I have to leave."

Vince nodded. "I can understand that." He stared at me while he chewed. "But you might want to consider that staying here with your grandma, living rent free for a while, is the perfect place to be while you get your work off the ground. No worries about being evicted, putting food on the table, keeping a car serviced for daily commutes." He shrugged. "Just sayin', it may be a really good setup."

I frowned. "Sounds like taking advantage. I don't wanna look like a mooch."

He shook his head. "Nah, it's family. You've been presented with a chance, best to take it. You never know what the future holds, but it won't hold much if you don't jump at opportunities."

Biting my lip, I thought over his words. "I already felt bad enough invading your space for a couple weeks. I can always stay at the inn."

Vince put his plate on the counter and stepped close to remove the plate from my hands and set it next to his. He cupped my chin. "Listen, this whole situation is completely foreign to me and I'm probably going to fuck it up."

My eyes went wide, but I kept quiet.

"Having you here has been great. I know it's only been a short time. Hell, maybe we'll realize we drive each other insane and eventually want to throw the other from the hilltop." His thumb caressed my lip. "For now? It's good and I like having you here. I like having you in my bed. I don't want to put any pressure on you—I'm not expecting marriage or forever—but I'd be happy to have you here for as long as you want to stay." He brushed a kiss over my lips and my knees instantly went weak. "I don't understand how I can feel such a connection with someone I just met, but I swear something clicked between us the moment you rolled down your window. I've *never* been in a position where I *wanted* to offer more than quick and easy to a guy. Cecil was one of those things that just kinda happened before I realized what was going on—looking back, I know now he stuck around for my name and nothing more." Vince pressed his forehead against mine. "I guess what I'm saying is I'm happy to have you here and I'm willing to just see where things go. If we end up fizzling out, so be it. I have no issues with finding a new place or just living together as friends."

I swallowed thickly and voiced a deeply buried wish I hadn't even had time to analyze. "And if we don't fizzle out?"

Vince smiled, nuzzling his nose against mine. "Then I guess we have a lot of fun ahead of us, huh?"

"You really feel it? This thing between us?" I whispered against his lips.

"Well, I definitely feel *something* between us," Vince teased as he rubbed his hard, thick cock against mine. "But yeah, I feel it. It's new and unfamiliar, but it's exciting—like a promise of something good."

I melted into him, pressing my mouth to the skin of his neck. "Are you willing to admit it's the Christmas magic?" I smiled into his neck.

"Let's not get carried away." Vince chuckled.

"Depending on who is doing what later tonight, I need a little prep time, but could I interest you in a little quickie on our lovely pile of blankets before a nap?" I rocked my hips into him.

Vince groaned and kissed me. "Never been so glad to have an old lady take my extra bed and couch," he mumbled as he wrapped me in his arms and walked me toward the living room.

We fell to the ground in a tangle of limbs, lips, and tongues. Sweatpants, shirts, and underwear were stripped off and I sighed my contentment when Vince settled between my spread thighs.

"Mary Joy has a very well-stocked hall closet," Vince murmured against my lips as he ground his cock against mine.

"Okay?" I wasn't sure where he was going with the statement.

"Random shit I always wondered about. It's like her own little pharmacy and toiletry supply store." He nipped at my lip before sliding his tongue over the sting. "Extra toothbrushes, soap, shower caps, and lotions—stuff you'd expect."

"Anything unexpected?" I trailed my hands down his back and gripped his ass.

"Not sure if it's unexpected or just randomly lucky, but she's got yeast infection cream, hemorrhoid wipes, lube, condoms, a multi-pack of douches, diapers, powdered formula, and pregnancy tests in there as well."

I couldn't help the snort laugh that escaped me. "Okay, now those really are some random items." I bit my lip. "I'm grateful for the lube and douches. Thoughts on the condoms?"

"Same. I meant it when I said I was vers. I know a lot of guys claim vers but then only want to top or bottom, but I'm down for both." He hooked his arms under my shoulders and rolled his hips, making me groan when our hot, hard shafts rubbed together. "I got tested right before moving here. Haven't had unprotected sex since and I've had two more full work-ups, all negative. So, with or without condoms, I'm good—I'll leave that one to you."

I tipped my head back and whimpered as he sucked on my collarbone before pressing open-mouthed kisses up my neck. "Negative here, too. Haven't been with anyone since my last test. Let's play it by ear and see how we feel tonight. I'm comfortable without if you are."

He nodded and returned to the moment. "Really wanna watch you come," Vince whispered in my ear as he rutted against me.

"Not gonna take much," I panted. "Touch me and I'll blow."

"Mmm, not yet." Vince continued to thrust our hard, leaking cocks together. "Tonight, I wanna tongue fuck that pretty ass of yours and work you open with my fingers before sliding deep inside."

"Fuck," I groaned. "Only if I get my turn on round two."

Vince growled. "Fuck yeah, wanna feel that gorgeous cock of yours stretch me open and fill me."

"Holy shit," I gasped. "Touch me, wanna come."

When Vince's fist closed around our throbbing cocks, I bit my lip and moaned.

"Good?" Vince murmured at my ear before turning his

gaze between our bodies to watch as our cocks fucked his fist. "Can you come like this? Wanna feel you against me."

"Yeah. Close. Oh fuck, so close." I pumped my hips, loving the steely heat of Vince's cock against mine as my balls drew up tight. "Fuck."

"Mmm, yeah, come for me, Kota," Vince whispered. "Wanna watch, wanna shoot all over you."

My orgasm washed through me as I shot my load over Vince's fingers and onto my belly. With a grunt, Vince exploded, his release mixing between us as we both rode out our pleasure. When we finally caught our breaths and came back to earth, Vince reached for a tissue box on the bottom shelf near our pallet.

We cleaned up quickly before Vince pulled me into his arms and yanked one of the blankets up to our shoulders. "Naptime," he murmured.

"We didn't watch a movie," I teased in protest even though sleep was quickly coming to claim me.

"We've got time. Sleep." Vince kissed my shoulder, the back of my neck, and my temple as the most perfect feeling washed over me. Safety, contentment, and hope blanketed me with just as much warmth as Vince's body wrapped around me. While my future was uncertain, I was positive that something good was headed my way.

Was a good dose of love and Christmas magic at play?

I wasn't sure, but I definitely wasn't going to turn it away.

Getting stuck in a snowstorm may have been just the lucky kickstart my life needed.

SIX

VINCE

I WOKE about an hour later and wondered for a moment where I was. Then my arms tightened around Kota and memories of what we'd done washed over me.

He was staying. At least for a while.

The sex had been amazing—better than anything I'd had in the past.

Having him in my space, talking to him, spending time with him—all things that would have irritated me with someone else—had me feeling all kinds of warm and cozy.

Happy.

Having Kota in my life made me happy.

I'd clearly lost my mind or wandered into an alternate universe because it was fucking ridiculous to feel this way about someone I just met.

If I let my head examine the situation, I couldn't help but roll my eyes. Kota was too young. He wasn't planning to stay forever. He and I barely knew each other. There was no reason to get attached and even less reason to allow myself to catch feelings.

But if I let my heart examine things, I was helpless

against the warmth that blanketed me and sent my feelings into excited overdrive. Kota and I fit together so perfectly. From that very first moment out on the road, we'd had some sort of connection I couldn't even explain. Sexually, there was no way to argue; the chemistry was amazing. But more than that—at my age, I knew without a doubt that sex wasn't everything—I'd loved every moment we'd spent together.

Maybe you're just lonely and any warm body would do.

I pressed my lips to Kota's bare shoulder and smiled when he stirred against me. Yeah, I could admit I'd been lonely. But I could have eased that loneliness by searching out a hookup if I'd wanted. Instead, Kota showed up and he'd been so much more than a random hookup from the start. Sure, we'd agreed early on that a holiday fling could be fun, but even when we thought it was meant to be short-lived, Kota had never felt like some meaningless hookup to me.

So, what? You think this kid wants to stay in this tiny Christmas town and weigh himself down with a washed-up, older man who has no big plans for his future other than teaching art classes and doing the occasional critique?

A week ago, I would have scoffed at the notion.

Now? It didn't seem so preposterous. Sure, Kota may eventually opt to leave, but he was there for the foreseeable future and I planned to do everything in my power to make Holly Hills be a place he never wanted to leave.

"Good nap?" Kota asked as he stretched and pressed his ass against my cock.

"Really good. You?"

"Yep." He shifted, rolling to face me, but his gaze traveled over my shoulder. "Oh my God, there's no other explanation. That's *got* to be the Christmas magic mixing with pheromones or something."

"Huh?" I rolled over so my back was to his front.

"Look at the plant. That thing was nearly dead yesterday

and now it looks even better than it did this morning. We've had sex out here twice; you can't tell me it's not feeding off that." Kota ran a hand down my bare chest and lower, his knuckles brushing through the short hair at my base and making my cock wake up.

I glanced up at the plant. Sure enough, it looked like it had come to life even more over the last several hours. "There is no way a plant came back to life because we had sex in front of it."

"You're right."

"I am?" I rolled my hips, eager to feel Kota's hand on my shaft.

"Yep, that's ridiculous." Kota kissed the sensitive skin where my neck and shoulder met. "However, whatever *this* might be between us, combined with—say it with me now —*Christmas magic*, could totally be the catalyst the plant needed."

I groaned and rolled my eyes, partly at the explanation, partly because Kota had wrapped his fingers around my dick and started to stroke. "So, you're trying to tell me the plant came to life through Christmas magic which is being powered by our mutual attraction and some lust-filled moments on a pile of blankets?" I couldn't keep the doubt from my words.

"Shhh," Kota whispered against my ear as he thumbed over my slit, "we don't question the Christmas magic."

I chuckled, but lost track of my argument as I thrust into his fist. "Keep doing that and I'll lose the ability to question everything."

Kota pressed his hard length against my ass and bit my shoulder. "That's my plan," he whispered.

We rocked together, his fist the perfect friction on my cock, his dick searching for release against my ass. When a slow, easy orgasm rolled through me and spilled over his fingers, I moaned as I reached back to pull him close to me, loving the warmth of his release against my skin.

"We really should get started on your website and business cards," I said with a groan. "If you seriously think two rounds are possible tonight, especially after *that*, you need to be doing some big-time wishing on that Christmas magic because my dick may never work properly again—it's not used to all this action."

Kota laughed and pressed a kiss to my neck. "Showers? Then we do some actual work. I still want a Christmas movie before bed." Kota rolled from the blankets. "Probably better wash this one. Pretty sure it's been soiled."

I snorted. "Probably."

Thirty minutes later, with a washer full of blanket and our hair wet from showers, Kota and I settled in at the office desk.

He had enough of a budget—especially since he was going to stay with Mary Joy for a while—that he was able to make sure he had a good domain name and a website that would be easy to update and user friendly.

"If you run into kinks, the customer service has really good reviews," I said. "Do you have any of your work on your phone or computer? You could start with contact information, a list of base prices for commissions, and a gallery of past work. Then we'll work on the business cards."

Kota set to work building his website and within a couple hours, fueled by cookies, hot chocolate, and coffee, he had it up and running. "I'll work on adding the actual store once I have works to sell." He grabbed a piece of paper and began to sketch something. When I realized it was a K, C, and S in an intricate design, I realized I'd been right about his talent. "What do you think about this as my logo? Put it on the business cards?"

"I think it's amazing. Can you get it from your paper to

your computer? That's beyond my technical skills. We need to print enough to hand out with any work Mary Joy sells, plus have some available for potential customers to pick up when they see your work she has displayed."

When Kota took a break to go to the restroom, I sat in awe of his talent as I scrolled through his new website on my phone. I had years and years' worth of contacts in the art community and I knew off the top of my head of at least five people who would be very interested in Kota's work, either as buyers or those looking to commission or contract his work. Clicking screenshots and excitedly sending samples of his work to the people I thought would be the most likely to bite, I felt a surge of pride that I could possibly provide such new and unique talent to the world of art while securing Kota an income.

Not to mention you think if he's making money he won't want to leave Holly Hills.

Selfishly, yes. But more than anything, I wanted Kota's work to get in front of the right people. Not for me—mostly —but for Kota's future. And if that future included me and Holly Hills, all the better.

As Kota returned and took his seat, I sent one last email to someone I thought *may* have had some kind of connection with an upscale boutique owner who was always looking for unique and one-of-a-kind pieces to provide for his clients. The worst that could happen was a no, but it was worth a shot.

For Kota.

By the time the website was to Kota's temporary satisfaction—we both knew he'd keep working on and improving it—and the business cards were printed with his logo, email, website, and phone number, it was dark and my stomach was empty.

"There's a loaf of homemade bread and some soup in the

kitchen. How's that sound for dinner?" I asked, pulling Kota from the desk chair.

"Delicious. You get it started and I'll find the movie. We can eat in front of the TV with the fire blazing." He bit his lip and gazed up at me, his jawline slightly pink from my scruff earlier. "And later…"

I gripped his chin and pressed a kiss to his lips. "Later, I'm taking you to my bed and giving the damn plant something to really get excited about."

Kota laughed, his head thrown back and blue eyes twinkling. "I'm going to make a believer of you yet."

"Don't get your hopes up," I said with a smack to his ass. But in reality, I was willing to claim Christmas was my favorite holiday and spout the truth of love and Christmas magic all over Holly Hills if it meant keeping Kota in my life.

We settled in to watch Christmas Vacation with steaming bowls of creamy broccoli cheddar soup and hunks of homemade bread.

Kota had been torn between Elf and Christmas Vacation, but we'd opted for the latter because I still had a bit of sap on the back of my hand. Despite washing and scrubbing, our tree adventure was still stuck on me.

"So, what type of art do you teach?" Kota asked as the movie played low and we savored soft bites of bread dipped in the cheesy soup.

"Depends. I have a class with all children one day a week, an adult class one day a week, and a mixed group one day a week." I blew on a bite of soup and swallowed it down before continuing. "Sometimes, if there are enough new members wanting to join, I'll do a Saturday basics class to get them on board and then slot them into the class that works best for them. Really, I do a lot of the same things in each class. The only real difference is which day of the week works best—and the adult class gets a little PG-13 from time to time with the older folks cracking jokes and innuendos."

"So, you're an artist? Is that what you did in your old job?"

Nosey little shit, I thought with a smirk.

"I know the basics of art and can apply them to drawing and painting, but I'm not an artist in the sense that you are."

Kota cocked his head. "What do you mean?"

"Whereas you come alive with your passion for your art, I simply know it—I enjoy it, but I don't live for it or want to crawl into it or feel as if I can finally breathe when I'm putting something on paper or canvas." I shrugged. "It's almost like someone who knows music history and music theory, but doesn't really play an instrument or feel music is their life's passion. Same for me, but with art. I know art history. I know fundamentals. I know what I'm looking for in pieces I like. But I'm not an artist in your sense. I observe and enjoy art, you live and breathe your skills and talents. I can teach the basic fundamentals and have a class painting a tree or sketching a bowl of fruit, but I'm not creating masterpieces."

Kota scoffed. "It's not like I'm creating masterpieces."

I reached for his hand and gripped it in mine. "Don't. Don't sell yourself short. I know good art when I see it and you're good. Maybe it's not the same as Picasso or Michelangelo, but you create beauty and that's all that matters. If you can take feelings and ideas and put them onto paper in such a way that brings people enjoyment, fulfillment, and satisfaction—in whatever ways that are unique to *them*—then you're creating masterpieces. Every single eye sees artwork slightly different. What I see in a piece is going to be different than what you see in a piece—

our experiences, our imaginations, our understanding of the world around us allow us to look at the exact same piece and get something completely different from it." With a kiss to his cheek, I continued. "I've seen your work. From your nature paintings and drawings to your geometric designs to the colorful water colors to the little charcoal drawings, you have more talent in your pinky than I've got in a whole forty-four years. Don't ever doubt that. There are people who will eat up your work and be lining up to commission pieces from you, I guarantee it."

Kota sighed. "From your mouth to God's ears. I do feel like—based on what I've seen of bigger names who do a lot of the same as me—that if I can spark some interest and grow my brand, a lot of people *will* want my work. I just feel like a little fish in a massive pond."

"The world of art *is* massive. Literature, music, paintings, sculptures, dance, poetry, the list goes on and on. Even if we focus down to *just* painting and drawing since those are your passions, it's still a vast field." I used the last bite of bread to mop up the remaining bit of soup before popping it in my mouth and swallowing. "But the good news is, just like readers are hungry for books from several authors and listeners devour music from a variety of artists, people who love art are almost always willing to—actively searching for it, in fact—buy art from artists they see as up-and-coming and unique. You have the uniqueness needed. I have a feeling that a client could give you the basis of an idea and you could make it come to life. And *that* is what people want. A lady who adores her dog but can't paint to save her soul—or doesn't have a desire to learn—would be thrilled to share pictures with you, tell you all about her dog's personality, and pay for a painting she can frame and keep forever."

Kota eyed me doubtfully. "I want to believe what you're saying, I really do, because it sounds like exactly what I've always wanted to do, but it's hard to think that people will really pay me for drawing or painting their pets or cars or whatever."

"They will. We just need to get your name out there and build your brand."

"I like the sound of that. I have a lot of ideas of things I could offer for commission projects." Kota reached for my bowl and stood.

"See, thinking like an artist *and* a businessman already. Perfect."

He gave me a shy smile as he walked the bowls to the kitchen.

When he returned, we settled onto our blankets to watch the rest of our movie, laughing and quoting lines as the holiday hilarity played.

The week before, I'd been going about my quiet, simple life not allowing myself to question my true happiness—I was more content in Holly Hills than I'd ever been anywhere so it seemed wrong to be greedy and want more than just contentment. I wasn't *unhappy*, but the moment Kota showed up in my life, it was like a light switch was flipped and I saw what I'd been missing.

Sure, maybe *any* guy who'd showed up would have filled a void, but deep down, I really didn't think it would have been the same. I'd never felt an instant spark toward anyone else in my life the way I did with Kota. Wrapped in his arms, laughing at a movie, sharing a meal, making plans, I'd honestly never felt so grounded and *right* in my entire life.

Was it fair to put all of that on Kota? Probably not. That's why I had to make sure I remembered he could leave at any point. Kota wasn't responsible for my happiness and I couldn't expect him to stick around just to keep me feeling better than I had in years.

However, I didn't see anything wrong with enjoying the

time we had together. He was staying at least for as long as it took to figure out if his art could earn him a living. We'd figure out the rest of it—the *us* part of it, if there was going to be an *us* outside of Holly Hills—later.

Would you leave this place for him?

I pushed away the thought. It wasn't something I was ready to consider. He had family here. If there was really something to the whole *Christmas magic* thing, he'd land a job that allowed him to do what he dreamed of doing while never having to leave Mary Joy.

Or me.

Yeah, I was a selfish bastard.

Kota shifted in my arms as the credits rolled. "You wanna hit the shower and meet me in about thirty or so minutes?"

I kissed his nose. "Perfect. I'm going to check to make sure there's water in the tree stand." Kota had warned me of the dangers of a tree getting too dry, so I wanted to be sure our pretty little tree hadn't sucked up all of its water already. "Go get that pretty ass prepped." I smacked his backside and smiled into his hair when he laughed.

Half an hour later, I walked into our room wrapped in a towel as I ran another towel through my dark, damp hair, only to find Kota conked out in bed.

Without even a hint of disappointment, I smiled as I took in his pale, creamy skin against the deep red sheets. A towel draped over his ass, hiding only one perfect cheek, while his damp hair flopped messily against the pillow.

Dropping my towel, I crawled into bed and tossed his towel to the floor before pulling the blankets up and over our bodies. Kota stirred, murmuring an apology for falling asleep, but I shushed him with a gentle kiss and wrapped him in my arms.

As a soft and easy slumber eased over me, I realized *this* was what was so different. I'd never in my life wanted to just spend time with a man. Never wanted to just laugh with him, talk with him, hold him in my arms. Then Kota waltzed in with his flirty, contagious smile, his passion, and his ridiculous talk about the magic of a holiday I'd sworn I despised, and I found myself completely satisfied to skip the sex and just hold him while we slept.

Christmas magic—if there even was such a thing, and I wasn't yet willing to admit I was maybe possibly starting to believe—was fucking up my head and my heart.

And I wasn't even mad.

SEVEN
KOTA

SOMETIME DURING THE NIGHT, I woke in Vince's arms and smiled sleepily against his chest. Exhaustion had finally caught up with me after my shower and I'd collapsed into bed thinking I'd just rest until Vince showed up. Clearly, that plan hadn't worked out too well.

The fact that Vince hadn't been angry or frustrated or even tried to coerce me into sex when he found me asleep bounced around in my head chattering away about how this one was different, this one was a keeper, this one deserved every good part of me.

It was still dark outside, but winter in the Midwest meant that it was dark until much later in the morning, so it was hard to tell what time it was. For a brief moment, I panicked, thinking I probably needed to get my ass out of bed, get busy on something, get over to Mary Joy's to help. But then I allowed myself to cuddle deeper into Vince's warm embrace and realized I had nowhere I had to be.

Yes, we had a tree to decorate, but it wasn't a mandate.

Yes, I wanted to go help Mary Joy, but I knew she wasn't

in too much of a rush. If she was even awake yet, she'd be enjoying her tea before tackling the day.

Yes, I needed to work on my site and some pieces, but I had time.

The snowstorm had forced me to slow down enough to realize I didn't *have* to rush back to the city and find another job I didn't love. Vince was right, Mary Joy had given me the gift of time and I'd be crazy not to use it.

For the first time in forever—if I let myself believe that *maybe* this whole independent artist thing could possibly work out—I felt calm and grounded. Like instead of needing to rush in to help and say hello before running away to a life I didn't really even think of as satisfying, I could now slow down and appreciate things a bit more.

I wanted to spend more time with Mary Joy. She wasn't getting any younger and I wanted to be around to help her. I *needed* to spend time with her to build memories that would comfort me down the road.

And as crazy as it sounded, I wanted to be around to see what happened between Vince and me. I *did* believe in Christmas magic and I was a sucker for a good love story— whoa, whoa, okay, *love* story was a bit too far…how about a good romance? —but even *I* was thinking the thing between Vince and me had happened way too quickly and easily. On the other hand, who was I to question something that was so easy and simple and felt so damn right?

I used to roll my eyes at stories of people who found their soulmate or met someone and felt as if everything in their life just clicked into place.

But then it happened to me and, after picking myself up from being knocked to the ground by the force of whatever was sparking between us, I realized it wasn't as ludicrous as I'd once thought.

Okay, yeah, it was still ludicrous. Who meets a stranger

one day and is seriously contemplating a future with them the next?

I ran my hand down Vince's back, loving the sparse, coarse hair under my hands and the soft curve of his ass. When he shifted, I pressed my hips against his and smiled to find him already hard.

"You trying to start something?" he asked gruffly, his breath hot against my ear.

"Maybe. If you're interested?"

"There's lube in the side table. I can grab the condoms if you want them." Vince's hands skimmed down my back and stopped on my ass as he gripped me and tugged me tightly against him.

"Lube, yes. Condoms, we've both been recently tested with negative results. If we're keeping this between just us while I'm here, I'm comfortable without them." My ass clenched at the thought of Vince's thick, bare cock breaching me.

He growled and rolled me to my back, settling between my legs as he kissed me within an inch of my life—seriously, the man could *kiss*. When he broke the contact, gasping, and began kissing, sucking, and biting his way down my body, I worried for a moment I'd blow before he even got to my ass. But Vince nuzzled his nose into the thatch of short hair at the base of my cock before licking up my shaft and swirling his tongue around my cock head. I fisted the sheets as he took me between his lips, the slick heat of his mouth sending fire coursing through my blood.

I whimpered when Vince let my rock-hard cock fall from his mouth, but when he positioned a pillow under my hips and nudged my legs farther apart, I couldn't complain.

"You okay with my tongue in your ass?" His breath on my sensitive skin sent shivers through me.

"Yeah, yes, fuck, please," I babbled.

Vince spread me open and licked a swipe from the cleft of my ass to my balls. Then he did it again, chuckling as I shuddered beneath him. He teased and twirled his tongue against my pucker, pressing into me with each pass as my body loosened to allow him entry. My hips bucked and I reveled in the way Vince gripped me and held me in place as he feasted on my ass.

"Fuck, need more, wanna feel you in me," I panted, my throbbing cock leaking on my stomach.

Vince reached for the lube in the drawer and the click of the lid mixed in the air with the sounds of our breathing and the scent of our sex. He smeared the slick liquid over my hole and slowly pressed into me with one finger. The initial intrusion made me gasp, but I immediately wanted more.

"Do another, it's so good," I begged.

He added a second finger and I found the stinging stretch I'd been expecting. I breathed through the sensation as Vince stilled. "You good?"

I nodded then managed a garbled "Yes," before losing myself to Vince's fingers in my ass. When he curled a finger and brushed over my prostate, I gripped my balls. "Fuck, too close. Want you in me."

Vince slowly removed his fingers and applied more lube, smearing his cock. "Where do you want to be?" he asked.

Coming back to myself enough to recall the fantasy I'd had in the shower about him fucking me bent over the mattress, I scrambled to the edge of the bed and stood up. "Over the side," I said as I faced the bed and bent over, my bare chest against the dark red sheets, my hard nipples an added sensation for my electrified body to deal with.

"God, you're gorgeous," Vince said, coming to stand between my spread legs. He ran a hand down my back, pausing at the small of my back, and I glanced over my shoulder.

We made a beautiful picture. My pale skin, Vince's more olive tone, my waiting ass, his glistening cock standing tall, his hand pressed to the small of my back as his eyes took me in.

"Spread your legs farther," he ordered, nudging them apart, exposing more of myself to him. "You want my fingers again?"

"No, fuck, no. Want your cock," I panted, fighting the urge to rut against the mattress, longing for release.

Vince stepped closer, pressing his thick shaft between my cheeks, the heat of his skin against mine sending a spark straight to my cock. He took himself in hand and tapped his cock head against my pucker. Then he pushed, slowly and gently.

I worked to breathe through the sting as the ring of muscle relaxed to allow Vince to sink deeper and deeper into me. "Fuck, you're thick," I murmured into the mattress.

"Too much? We can stop," Vince said, pausing in his forward movement.

"Don't you dare," I warned. "It's so good."

"Too good," Vince bit out as he sank the last bit into me, his balls flush against my skin. "Just a warning that this won't last long."

"Mmmm, go for it. Don't care how long, just wanna feel you."

Vince started with a slow rhythm, his thrusts long and deep as he gripped my hips. His cock head brushed over the bundle of nerves deep inside with each thrust and I knew I needed to feel him harder and faster.

"Harder," I said. "You don't have to be gentle."

Vince shifted, bringing his chest to my back as he whispered in my ear. "Maybe I like it gentle. Maybe I wanna fuck you slowly until you come apart under me."

I nearly lost myself when Vince reached for my hands and

entwined our fingers against the red sheets. "I don't care if it's slow or fast, I just wanna feel you come in my ass. My cock is about to explode."

Vince chuckled, biting at my ear, but he increased his rhythm. As his hips thrust hard and fast, he kissed my neck and whispered in my ear telling me how hot and tight and good I was.

I untangled my right hand from his and reached under my body to stroke my cock. "Fuck, Vince, gonna come."

"Do it, wanna feel this hot ass come on my cock," Vince demanded as his thrusts faltered. "Fuck, I'm so close."

With a final stroke, I shot my load, my ass clenching around Vince right before his cock stilled deep inside, pumping me full of his hot release.

After a moment of catching our breaths, I shifted to ease a cramp in my leg and Vince eased out slowly.

"Here," he said as he tossed me the towel from the night before, "wipe up. We've got a bit more time to sleep."

I cleaned myself the best I could and wiped up the mess I'd left on the edge of the bed. "What time is it?"

"Early enough that we can sleep before we even have to consider getting up. Guarantee Mary Joy isn't even up yet." Vince finished wiping off with the towel and crawled into bed. "Come here, I'll protect you from the wet spot." He yanked my hand and pulled me on top of him as I laughed.

I slipped from on top of him and cuddled into his warm embrace. "Mmm, I can definitely do with more sleep. Maybe when we wake up, we can go again," I mumbled against his chest.

Vince chuckled. "Better hope the Christmas magic fairy comes and does a number on my dick before then because it's demanding a week-long vacation and compensation pay after meeting you."

I laughed—something I'd realized I hadn't done much of

lately until I met Vince—and patted his ass. "Or you could just give me this ass and let me do all the work. Your worn-out dick doesn't even have to come to the party."

He groaned. "Give me a couple hours of sleep. If your mouth or cock are coming anywhere near my ass, my dick is going to want to join the fun. He needs to rehab for a moment."

I lifted my face to press a kiss against Vince's lips, but he slowed the contact and deepened the kiss. Our tongues mated in a slick, sensual dance and my heart caught in my throat. This was—different? New? Better? Unspoken words and emotions passed through that kiss and I knew I'd never be the same after meeting Vince Carter. Whether this was a passing fling we'd both look back on fondly—and God, I didn't want it to be just a memory—or the beginning of a gorgeous life story we'd tell people for years to come, I knew without a doubt that Vince had changed me.

The kiss turned sleepy and soft until we drifted off in each other's arms.

When I cracked an eye open sometime later, the room was slightly brighter with the somber morning light of a dawning winter day. We'd shifted in our sleep and Vince's back was to my front, his ass slotted perfectly against my cock.

Moving my arm over his body and pressing a hand against his chest, I savored the quiet moment. Was I just enjoying time away from a shitty job and a lackluster relationship or were my crazy thoughts about waking up with Vince every day for the rest of my life valid and real? Holding him close, feeling his heartbeat under my palm, our bodies pressed together as if they'd finally found their home, I had no doubt this was about more than just needing a break from reality.

And I wanted it. Wanted the possibility of what Vince and I could have together.

"You thinking serious thoughts? Or planning your attack on my ass?" Vince asked as he pushed against me.

Skimming my hand down his chest, I caressed my knuckles over his semi-erect cock. "Combo of both."

"Wanna tell me about it?" Vince placed his hand on top of mine and stroked his shaft with me.

"Nah, the serious is way too soon—I'd look like a fool. And the ass attack is supposed to be a smooth operation—I can't let you in on the plan."

Vince twisted slightly and pulled my head close so our lips were nearly touching. "Just know, in terms of the serious side of things, we can look like fools together. I don't understand any of it—it defies logic—but there's no way I'd want to miss out on whatever it is." He pressed a kiss to my lips. "Now, I'm going to act surprised, but I believe you have an ass to invade."

"Roll over."

Vince rolled to his stomach and I knelt between his legs, lifting his hips to shove a pillow under him. Reaching for the lube and tossing it on the mattress for later, I shifted to my belly and pressed kisses against Vince's ass as he groaned. When I spread his cheeks and swiped my tongue over his entrance, his whole body shuddered and my cock twitched in anticipation.

After licking, teasing, swirling, and fucking his ass with my tongue, I grabbed the lube. "Fingers okay?"

Vince grunted and rocked his hips. "Just long enough to stretch me, want you inside before I come."

"I like that plan," I said, smiling as I slicked my fingers before smearing the lube around his hole.

Pressing gently against his entrance, I slowly worked his muscle until my finger slid in easily.

"Oh God," Vince groaned. "Do another one."

Not wanting to move too quickly, but knowing we were

both desperate to get to the part where I buried myself deep inside, I added a second finger. Vince's body stilled with his hiss and I paused. "You okay?"

He took a deep breath and rocked his ass on my fingers. "It's so good. Just took a minute."

I slid both fingers in and out, the slick heat of Vince's body toying with me as I imagined sinking my dick into him.

"Fuck, it's too much, want more," Vince rutted against the pillow under his hips.

"Another finger?" I offered, knowing he didn't want another finger.

"No, damn it. Need your cock."

I chuckled as my fingers slid from his heat. "And here you were worried you wouldn't be able to go again. We're discovering your secret super powers."

"My ass is totally on board. Even my dick is attempting to play—he may just not have much to offer at the grand finale." Vince moved to his hands and knees, tossing the pillow to the side.

"This way good for you?" I asked, caressing his ass from my position between his spread legs.

"Yeah," Vince said, dropping to his elbows.

Taking my leaking cock in hand, I pressed against his pucker and gritted my teeth as his tight heat yielded to my entry. "Oh fuck. Fuuuck," I groaned as his body drew me in. I rubbed the small of Vince's back as I worked my length into him. When my balls pressed against his skin, I paused, hands on his hips, thumbs tracing circles on his lower back. "You good?"

Vince's fists clenched the sheets. "So fucking good. God damn, you feel so fucking perfect. Move, wanna feel you come in me."

I began a slow, steady thrusting as Vince's tight channel adjusted to my presence. With each thrust, my body declared nothing had ever been as good, nothing would ever compare, and nothing would ever be the same. Increasing my speed, loving the press of my balls on his, our skin slapping together, I leaned over and kissed Vince's back.

"Can you go if I drop down?" Vince asked.

"You feel so fucking good, I can go however you need me to."

Vince lowered himself to his stomach, legs spread, and I entered him again as my body pressed against his, chest to back, my hips grinding and rolling.

"Shit, Kota, I'm close. You're so damn good."

"Do it," I demanded. "Come for me. Wanna feel it from inside."

Vince reached to jack his cock and a shuddering orgasm rolled through him, gripping my cock from within.

My balls drew up tight and I thrust once, twice, three more times as the release washed over me and I spilled deep in Vince's ass before collapsing onto him with a groan. "Fuck, I think even I might need a break after that. I'm not sure my body has anymore cum to come."

Vince chuckled. "I definitely depleted my main reserves and then some."

"We can build our supply back up at Mary Joy's." I wrinkled my nose. "Ewww, talking about building up my cum supply at my grandma's house is gross. Let's never speak of it again."

Vince laughed. "You're the one who brought it up. These sheets need washed and I'm starving."

"Not to mention *we* need washing. Showers, breakfast, tree decorating, and then we head to Mary Joy's?" I rolled from atop his body and faced him.

"Perfect. You want hot chocolate?"

"Does Christmas magic exist?" I asked, cocking a brow.

Vince narrowed his eyes.

"*Yes*, I want hot chocolate." I kissed him. "And *yes*, Christmas magic is real."

He chuckled. "I'm not ready to commit to anything just yet."

But the sparkle in his eyes and the warmth between us—the inexplicable emotional connection we shared—hinted that Vince was maybe a bit closer to believing in love and Christmas magic. Not only that it existed, but that he deserved a bit of both.

EIGHT

VINCE

AS WE DECORATED THE TREE, I realized with an oddly easy acceptance that I was willing to do whatever it took to spend the rest of my life making Kota as happy as he was when stringing garland around a pine tree.

It didn't make any sense. Outside of spending three days laughing with him and knowing him intimately, there was no reason we should have worked together. But we did and it felt so right. I'd gone from a man who rolled my eyes and scoffed when others spoke of finding their soulmates and knowing within minutes they wanted to spend the rest of their life with that person, to being a man swamped in a mixture of disbelief and certainty that Kota was my person.

"Ohhh, look at these," Kota exclaimed as he took delicate glass icicles from a box of ornaments. "Do you think the tree has too much already?"

I stood back and studied the tree, my arms crossed over my chest. "No, those are tiny, they won't be too much. Go for it." Honestly, I would have gone and chopped down another tree in a heartbeat if Kota had wanted to decorate more.

With what should have been a gaudy and exorbitant amount of Christmas décor on the tree and around the house, we tidied up and packed away boxes for whenever we decided to take the decorations down.

"Go ahead," Kota said, pointing at the Christmas cactus, "try to tell me you don't believe in the power of love and Christmas magic."

The plant had transformed from nearly dead to perky, green, pink, and gorgeous. And I'd done absolutely nothing aside from bringing Kota into my home and falling for him.

Was what we had love?

I wanted to scoff and protest that I was too old and that ship had sailed. But my heart beat differently around Kota and I couldn't be so sure. Maybe what we had *was* love and I was just slow to recognize it because I'd never experienced anything like it.

Was Christmas magic in the air?

I thought about how much had changed since the moment I found Kota in the ditch—the plant, the warmth in my heart, the feeling that everything was *right*, the sparkle in Kota's eyes, the hopeful happiness in his smile.

Maybe the magic was yet one more thing I couldn't explain and would never fully understand, but I had to admit there was definitely something at play.

"Fine. Thank you, Christmas magic, for bringing my plant back from the brink of death." I huffed and gestured toward the plant, biting back a smile.

Kota grinned and wrapped his arms around me. "Thank you, Christmas magic, for careening my car into an icy ditch and stranding me with a hot-as-sin, sexy man with only one bed."

I snorted. "We'll have to thank Mary Joy for that."

Kota rolled his eyes. "No, let's not give her any fodder for her meddling."

We bundled up and made our way through the snow to the garage where I got the ATV started and let it warm up for a bit while I grabbed a shovel and made a path back to the porch. Kota pilfered through boxes in the garage as I worked, making a stack of frames and what appeared to be shadow boxes.

"You ready to go?" I asked as I put away the shovel.

"Yep, show me how to ride this beast," Kota teased.

I rolled my eyes and swung a leg over the ATV. "Pretty sure you know exactly how to *ride*. Climb on."

"Mmm, love that invitation. Save it for later when I can climb on and ride *you*," Kota whispered in my ear as he situated himself behind me.

The day was bright and sunny, the snow blinding even through our sunglasses as we made our way slowly toward the Amaryllis with the snow plow attachment assisting in our journey. Kota's gloved hands curled into my coat pockets as he watched the landscape slide by.

When we reached the bed-and-breakfast, I dropped Kota at the door and told him to go on in. I wanted to clear a few paths that might be needed—although, it was likely still going to be a day or two before the county got any trucks up the hill to dig us out. Holly Hills had a few citizens with snow blades they could attach to their trucks, but snow as deep as we were dealing with would take some time to clear for sure.

By the time I parked the ATV and climbed the steps to the backdoor of the inn, I was more than ready for a hot fire, a warm drink, and maybe some lunch. I knocked snow from my boots and stripped out of my cold weather gear before wandering to the kitchen to find Kota and Mary Joy deep in discussion about his plans.

"Well, I'll be cheering you on. And you know I'll share your work and your site with anyone and everyone who will listen. I've also got several friends from way back who I still keep in contact with—they're located all over the country and I know without a doubt that they are interested in art or have friends who are—I'll be sure to send your info their way." Mary Joy stood and straightened her apron. "Get your social media set up. I'll blast your site and your other platforms from my personal account and the Amaryllis account." She patted Kota's cheek. "I know this doesn't mean you're staying forever, but I'm thrilled to have you here while you get your feet under you. I think you've got something special and you can really make a go of this idea. Whether you settle in to do it from here or elsewhere, I want nothing but the best for you. Now, if I get a vote, I say you stay here; we'd love to have you."

Kota hugged his grandma and smiled at me over her shoulder. "Thanks, that means a lot. I'm not committing to forever, but I think I can safely say I'll be here for at least a while. Can I go find those canvases and supplies you bought last year?"

"Of course." Mary Joy nodded toward the back stairs. "They should be in the upstairs corner closet in a box labeled Kota Christopher."

As soon as Kota's footsteps disappeared up the stairs, Mary Joy turned to me with a gleam in her eyes. "You seem happy. Kota seems happy. I do suspect those two things are related."

I smirked, knowing she was digging. "What's not to be happy about? We have a warm house, good food, family and friends, and Christmas right around the corner."

She narrowed her eyes, but a smile teased at her lips. "Well, not only are love and Christmas magic hard at work, I do believe a holiday miracle has taken place." She held my chin and studied me. "Do you mean to tell me that Vince

Carter—self-proclaimed Christmas grump and non-believer in Christmas magic—has come around and allowed himself to see the joy in the holiday season?"

I rolled my eyes with a huff and moved from her gaze. "I'm just saying that I have a lot to be grateful for and I'm done trying to pretend I don't want or deserve that happiness. This is a good place, I have a good life. I'm willing to admit that there's a lot of good out there and I'm not going to hide from it anymore."

Mary Joy cocked her head. "And does my grandson have something to do with this?"

Realizing there was absolutely no reason to deny it, I shrugged. "Probably?" I ran my hand through my hair and gripped the back of my neck. "Yeah, he does. He absolutely *shouldn't*, but he does. I knew he was good guy based on what you had told me, but I wasn't prepared for the sucker punch fate landed on me the moment I met him. He's…" I bit my lip and stared at the stairway where Kota had disappeared, "special. Like no one I've ever met. Which is crazy because he's just a regular guy, but there's this ridiculous connection between us and I'm helpless to fight it."

Mary Joy smiled broadly. "That's the exact same thing I felt for his grandfather. When I met Chris, I was nearly bowled over with the absurdity of how drawn I was to this man who should have felt like a complete stranger, but instead made my heart feel as if it had finally met its other half."

"Yeah, that's exactly it." I sighed. "At least you and Chris were close to the same age. Don't you think it's a bit weird there's like twenty years difference between me and Kota? Shouldn't you be freaked out by it?"

"Stuff and nonsense." Mary Joy waved her hand. "If he was ten and you were thirty, sure. But you're both grown men, you can make your own decisions about who you're attracted to." She raised a brow. "Is something else bothering you?"

I shrugged. "Just thinking about how my family was so adamant that I was an abomination—bet they'd cast me even further into the depths of hell if they knew I'd gone and fallen in love with a man twenty years my junior."

Mary Joy's eyes widened. "I prefer to stick to the positives —which I'll do in just a moment—but it needs to be said. Your parents were rotten excuses for human beings. There is not a single thing wrong with you or Kota and I'll spend the rest of my years making sure you both know how cherished and special you are."

I sniffed, trying to ease the burning in my nose and throat.

"Now, for the positives, did you just say you're in love with my grandson?"

Pacing the kitchen, I ran my hands through my hair. "Ugh, yes? Maybe? I don't know! I've never been in love. Never thought it was for me—truly, never thought I was made for it or deserved it."

"But now?"

"How can I love a man I just met?"

"Does he feel like a stranger?" Mary Joy asked.

I thought of the laughter we'd shared, the warmth of his body against mine, and the ease at which we fell into something uniquely *us*. I shook my head. "No. He feels like someone I've been waiting for my entire life."

"Then don't question it. You've been given a gift. Nurture it, cherish it, and protect it."

"What if he leaves and I'm left with nothing but devastation?" I spoke the words I hadn't been willing to admit were weighing heavy on my heart.

"If you love him—and he'll have you—what would keep you here if he decides he needs to work elsewhere?" she asked.

I opened my mouth to protest. This was my home. I was happy here. I was needed. But every word would have been an empty excuse. My home was where my heart was. My happiness wasn't reliant on a place. And what I did for the people of Holly Hills could be replaced if I took my skills elsewhere. Just like Kota hoped to be able to work from anywhere, I could also work from wherever I needed.

"That's what I thought." Mary Joy nodded. "My wish is for him to find success and happiness and fulfillment in his art and business so he can stay here if that's what he needs. But if he needs to leave, there's nothing holding you here."

"Gee, thanks," I deadpanned.

"You know we adore you and wouldn't ever *want* you to leave. But this town understands the unexplainable and how the heart gets what the heart wants—even when it's not what we realized we needed. You'd be missed, but it would be accepted." She began to pull lunch items from the fridge. "You've seen his work? You think he has something unique to make this business thing happen?"

I nodded. "I do. I haven't heard back yet, but I'm hoping some of my contacts in the art community will come through with some leads for him."

Mary Joy raised her brow. "What do you mean?"

"I sent some samples of his work to a few people I know in hopes of him getting some bites for commissions and contracts."

"That was very kind of you, I'm sure Kota was touched you did that."

I shuffled my feet. "Well, it was kinda a spur of the moment decision so I didn't really tell him about it."

She pursed her lips. "You sent samples of his work without his knowledge?"

"Just some screenshots of things he was putting on his website."

"Maybe you should tell him?" she suggested.

"Nothing may come from it. No reason to bring anything up and then have it not pan out."

Mary Joy crossed her arms over her chest. "I know I wasn't meant to find out who you were in your past life and I've kept that secret without fail. But don't you think that an *artist* would possibly want to know the man he's getting involved with is a big-time art critic?"

"We've barely just met," I said, my hackles rising. "It's not like there's been a lot of time to tell him."

She narrowed her eyes. "Time enough to take him to bed, but not enough to let him know exactly who you are?" When my cheeks pinked and my eyes widened, Mary Joy rolled her eyes. "I wasn't born yesterday, I know that look I saw between the two of you."

I huffed out a breath. "Last time someone knew who I was, they used me to get ahead in the world of art and it nearly ruined my reputation. Pardon me for finding comfort in the fact that Kota likes me for *me* and not my name."

Mary Joy's face softened. "I hear you and I understand, I do. I'm just saying that he may be hurt that you went behind his back. And he's not going to understand why you'd hide your identity from him."

"I'm Vince to him. I'm Vince to most people I care about these days. Alan Vincent exists, but in a completely different world."

She nodded as she studied me. "A different world, but a world Kota wants to be a part of. Hiding the truth may hurt you. And just like you don't want to think someone is with you just for your name, I'm pretty sure Kota doesn't want to get a foot in the door just because the man he's sleeping with put in a good word for him."

I winced. Was that all I was for Kota? Just the guy he was sleeping with? We'd started out as a holiday fling, maybe that's all we were.

Footsteps sounded down the stairs.

Mary Joy gave me a look. "It's best to come clean now."

I shook my head. There was no reason just yet. If nothing came from the feelers I'd sent out, Kota wouldn't need to know.

What? You just planning on building something with the guy and never telling him you still do critiques under a very high-profile name?

I pushed away the thought. I'd quit the critiques if needed. The main thing for me was knowing Kota was with me for me and not because of who I used to be—who I still was in some ways. I was no longer involved in the center of the art world—I hung out like a recluse on the outer edges only because some people still valued my eye and my opinion. I didn't *need* that. Not the way I needed Kota.

"Wow, you stocked up," Kota announced as he came around the corner. "I'm going to take inventory later and put in an order for things I might need. Mmmm, is that lunch?"

We helped Mary Joy prepare food for the guests and serve them in the dining room before the three of us took our lunch in the kitchen. She promised her guests a movie and charades later on, but they'd have to excuse her while she doted on her grandson.

"I'm thinking we should make some pies," Mary Joy stated as we cleared our dishes.

The two girls from town who'd offered to stay on at the Amaryllis to help through the season were carrying lunch dishes from the dining room and stacking them next to the sink.

"Butterscotch?" Kota asked, a hopeful gleam in his eyes.

"Butterscotch, cherry, and..." Mary Joy glanced my way. "Vince, you've had several of my pies, what's your choice?"

"Peach with the crumble topping, no question."

"Ohhhh, that sounds so good," Kota agreed.

"Nope, you committed to butterscotch," I teased. "No cutting in on my peach."

"Actually, let's do two butterscotch pies—one for Kota to take home—and the cherry and peach can be crumbles instead. Easier and makes more, plus the guests always love the crumbles." Mary Joy dried her hands on her apron. "Ladies, if you can finish up the dishes, I'll gather the ingredients. After lunch is cleaned up, I need you to take care of the laundry and spot clean the bathrooms, please." She turned to us. "Boys, can you go out to the barn and bring in two jars of peaches and two jars of tart cherries? And grab some firewood on your way in, please. Kota, if you're able, I'd love to have you make a few quick pieces and leave them here with your cards. Over the next few days, maybe you can make some more pieces, add them to your online gallery as examples, and display them here at the inn to pique interest."

"Sounds good. I'm going to get some blank greeting cards and see about making original series of artwork on cards. Like a box of twelve each with a different piece of work focused on the same theme." Kota shrugged into his coat.

"That sounds wonderful. The art of sending cards and letters has gone to the wayside, but I know several people who adore having unique greeting cards available to send. Maybe think about ways to add your work to stationery?"

Kota nodded. "I like that idea. Notepads, cards, sticky notes, notebooks, stickers, stamps..." he trailed off. "I actually *love* that idea. I just wish I could get someone already in that field to assist in the next steps. I know I've got the right kind of artwork, I just need the production and distribution portion to fall into place."

I didn't want to get his hopes up, but I *knew* I had contacts with the right connections to make Kota's plans happen easier than they would on his own. I'd keep my fingers crossed the connections were made.

Hell, I'd even hope for a little Christmas magic to come through and make it happen.

We piled into our coats, gloves, hats, and boots and made our way to the barn.

"Why'd she send us all the way to the barn? It's so damn cold," Kota mumbled.

"Likely doesn't want to deplete her food store in the basement when she's got us here to fetch jars of fruit for her. We'll be quick. Won't be *warm* in the barn, but it shouldn't be *as* cold." I opened the side door of the old barn and waited for Kota to walk in before closing it behind us.

Once our eyes adjusted to the darkness, Kota sighed.

"Wow, this brings back so many memories. I used to play in here all the time when I'd come visit as a kid. Even the smell is the same." Kota walked toward the shelves against the wall. "You know, I remember now why she uses the barn stores first. She puts most of her canning in the basement where it's cool, but the overflow comes out here. She uses it first because she prefers her fruits and veggies jars stay cool rather than getting warm in a hot summer barn."

"That makes sense. She had me sturdy up those shelves the first summer I was here. Said she was always afraid they'd topple over. Have you been in here lately?" I turned on the battery-powered lantern near the workbench.

"No, not since I was a kid. The last few times I came to visit, I didn't have any reason to come out here." Kota gazed around the wide, open barn. "Wow, where did all of this stuff come from?"

"The workbench and tools are mostly mine, a few things leftover from your grandpa I think. The pallets are ones she's collected—I think she was hoping to do something artistic with them, but hasn't gotten around to it. The old sleds are also part of her collection. The rest is just odds and ends she or I have picked up from sales and auctions and flea markets."

Kota walked through the organized collection of items and whistled. "Do you think she'd mind if I used some of these? I just had a great idea for some pieces—I think residents here would really love them."

"I think she'd rather you use them than let them sit here gathering dust. Get the jars. We'll grab firewood and then drive the ATV back to carry whatever you need."

We delivered the jars of fruit and firewood and Kota asked if he could use some of the pallets and sleds in the barn.

Of course, Mary Joy obliged and we headed back out to load the ATV.

After climbing off the vehicle and walking toward the barn, something hit the back of my head with an icy thump followed by a cackle of laughter. I turned to see Kota beaming as he formed another snowball.

"I wouldn't do that if I were you," I warned as I bent to pick up my own icy weapon and packed it into a solid ball.

"Oh yeah," Kota taunted, "what are you going to do about it?"

He let his snowball fly, hitting me right in the chest and I hurled one at him as I gave chase.

Kota yelped and ran, but the snow outside of the little path was deep and hard to run in. I lunged and toppled him to the ground as snow encased us.

Stretched out on our sides, bright smiles and cold noses, Kota and I laughed together.

"This isn't nearly as romantic as they make it look in those cheesy holiday movies," Kota mused.

"Of course not," I agreed. "To be at our most cheesy, we need to make snow angels, have a snowball fight, and fall to the ground with a near kiss before we're interrupted by some well-intentioned family member."

"It's way too deep for snow angels. I tried the snowball fight—which I won, by the way."

"We've fallen to the ground," I murmured, leaning in close and brushing my lips over his, "but I think we're far past the near kiss part."

"And it's way too cold and wet for any kind of hanky panky in the snow," Kota said, pressing a hard and fast kiss to my lips.

"Boys?" Mary Joy's voice danced over the piles of snow. "Boys? You okay?"

Kota snorted. "And there's the well-intentioned family member."

"Maybe we *do* have our own version of a cheesy holiday movie," I said as I stood and pulled him up, waving to Mary Joy.

She returned the wave and headed back inside.

"Yeah, but our cheesy holiday movie is a lot steamier than any I've ever seen—at least on network TV," Kota said with a smile as he leaned in to kiss me again.

"Also, did you just say hanky panky?" I teased as we headed toward the barn.

Kota chuckled. "Yeah, I can remember my grandma saying that to my parents when I was little. I never understood what it meant. Then, once I knew what it meant, I didn't ever want to think of the phrase in association with my parents."

"Yeah, parent hanky panky is a huge no." I shuddered. "I truly wondered sometimes just how I came to be. If you knew my parents...I just wonder how they ever ended up getting frisky enough to get pregnant. It had to be lights off, clothes mostly on, no romance, and highly unfulfilling."

Kota snorted. "Well, as much as it may scar you to think about it, I'm glad they did the deed at least once." He winked. "Who knows, maybe your mom was a wild cat in bed and your dad was like her sub."

"Oh my God, stop," I said, picking up snow and smashing it on his head. "You've contaminated my brain and I'll never be the same. Oh God, I might puke."

Kota laughed as he shook the snow from his hat and walked into the barn. "We can rinse it all away tonight. Pretty sure you invited me to climb on and ride before and I'm taking advantage of that once we're back home."

I yanked him close and pressed his back against the barn wall. "I'll hold you to that," I growled before crushing a kiss against his lips.

When we broke apart, Kota's lips and cheeks pink from the cold and the kiss, his icy blue eyes sparkling, he blinked a couple times before biting his lip.

"What?" I asked.

"What is this?" he asked. "I'm okay with it being just a holiday fling and moving on—but I'd be lying if I said I didn't want it to be more. I know it's way too soon and it doesn't make sense, but I'm already in too deep. If we're going to enjoy this for a while and then say see ya, I need to know so I can prepare myself."

Pressing my forehead against his, I sighed. "As much as we probably *should* have our fun and say goodbye, I don't think I can. I'm not saying either of us should commit to forever, but I'd like to see where things go. You're staying for a while. Maybe we see where we are if and when you decide to leave."

"This question is probably unfair, but would you ever consider leaving with me?"

My breath caught in my throat.

"No, you know what, don't answer that. We have now. We have at least until I decide what the hell I'm doing with my life. We can reassess then." Kota pressed a kiss to my lips. "Let's load these things up and get back to the inn. I'm freezing."

NINE
KOTA

"TELL me what you want to do with the pallets and sleds," Mary Joy said as she busied herself making pies and crumbles.

"Can I help with anything?" I asked, feeling guilty to just be sitting at the table sipping hot chocolate while she worked.

"I'm eighty, not dead. I've been running a kitchen almost three times as long as you've been alive. I can handle a dang pie crust." She waved a rolling pin my way.

I sighed and held up my hands. "Sorry, it's just, I came here thinking you were dying and I thought I was going to be helpful and make your dying wish come true. I feel kinda useless now."

Grandma snorted. "Sorry to disappoint. You'll be dealing with me for several more years if I have my way. I'm sorry I got you here under unintentionally false pretenses, but I can't say it wasn't for the best. My wish will always be for you to be here in Holly Hills. Now, tell me about the pallets and sleds."

Vince rubbed my knee under the table as he sipped his

coffee and scrolled through his phone. "He's got some great ideas. I think we'll need to keep an eye out for more when we're at flea markets."

Knowing that Vince thought my art was good and worthy of possibly selling made my chest fill with a warm pride. Maybe he was just one person, but it meant a lot.

"So, with the sleds, I was thinking I could get them cleaned up. Some I could leave looking rustic, some I could paint and varnish to look new. Then I wanted to paint scenes on them—probably winter or holiday images. They could be used for decoration on a porch or something." Ideas always seemed so great in my head, but the moment I tried to explain them aloud they sounded ridiculous.

"I love it. I want the first one. I'll put it on the porch. When guests ask about it, I'll tell them where I got it. If you're working from here, you can sell directly to them." Mary Joy finished rolling the pie crust and gently placed it in the pan.

"For the pallets, I was thinking of doing scenes on those, too. The idea I was toying with was to have a set of two. On each side, there's a seasonal scene. They can be displayed for each season. I'd also do some individual ones, but I really love the idea of the set."

"I love that idea even more—and I know I'm supposed to encourage you in all things because I'm your family, but I'm not just blowing smoke up your ass, I really do think these are amazing ideas." She poked holes in the pie crusts and put them in the oven while she started the butterscotch mixture with brown sugar, milk, and butter. "Not to be greedy, but make the first set for me. I've got the perfect place for a pallet to be displayed out front, leaning against the flag pole in that flower garden. It will be the perfect conversation starter with guests—you have no idea how often people are asking me where I bought certain things. I'll be able to send them straight to you."

Vince cleared his throat. "One thing we're going to need to think about is delivery and shipping. Here in town, it won't be a problem. If guests want to buy and take items with them, that's the easiest. But if they don't have room—or if someone from out of town orders online—we need to price packaging and shipping options." He tapped his fingers on the table. "Could get really expensive. Maybe we think about pick-up only—or we make a radius of fifty miles around Holly Hills and we'll deliver for a fee."

I blinked slowly, considering his words. He was damn smart and I loved that he was already talking as if I'd get a lot of orders. But what I really loved was that he referred to this next step with *we*. It warmed my heart to know he'd so seamlessly fallen into place with my plans.

Yeah, yeah, it was still totally crazy that we'd known each other such a short time and were already referring to things as if we were a long-term couple—and before being in the situation, I would have told people it was ridiculous and not a good idea to get so real and serious with someone they just met. But nothing about what Vince and I shared felt wrong.

Kinda weird? All kinds of giddy? A little like floating on air? Maybe even a bit life changing?

Yes. Yes, to all of that.

But bad? Wrong? Sending up red flags?

Not at all.

Honestly, I'd felt unease, uncertainty, apprehension—truly, a gut-deep sense of dread—when I'd started my first week at my old company. I liked to think my gut had never really steered me astray.

Don't get me wrong—I was an idiot for staying at the job for as long as I did. Seriously, those are bits of my soul sucked away that I may never get back.

But my *point*...I didn't feel anything bad in my gut about Vince.

"That's a really good idea. You could make a day trip of it. Maybe even consider widening the radius to one hundred miles for an additional fee. I still think that would be cheaper than trying to ship—at least in these beginning stages." Mary Joy stirred the butterscotch filling as it bubbled on the stove. "Gather up orders and you could deliver over the course of a few days—take Vince's truck or the old RV, she's nothing fancy but she runs. See some sights, stay in some unique places—giving me all the intel of course—and maybe gather inspiration for your work. Who knows, you may even find places that would be interested in selling your work if you could deliver it to them."

With visions of a successful future, I finished my hot chocolate and wandered to Grandma's back room to work on some pieces while Vince puttered around the house and the barn working on odds and ends.

Several hours later, I had a fun little mixture of nature scenes, animals, cartoon-ish creatures, and bold geometric designs on several canvases. They weren't my most elaborate or difficult pieces, but I thought they gave a good representation of what I was capable of. I'd also made a few little four-packs of greeting cards with some cardstock I'd found in the closet. Everything I'd worked on was meant to pique interest, get people asking about the work, and make a connection. Once my business information was in their hands, I had a much better chance of them ordering pieces or inquiring about commissions.

Later, as the three of us wrapped up some delightful visits with guests and Vince and I helped Mary Joy clean up the kitchen, she spoke of the next couple weeks leading up to Christmas.

"It's crazy to me how many people are interested in

traveling and staying in a bed-n-breakfast during the holidays, but if they want a place to stay, I'm going to provide it." She shrugged and dried a bowl before putting it in the cabinet.

"What kind of help do you need from us?" Vince asked.

"Well, I plan to use Kendra and Stacy as much as possible because I know they can use the extra money, but I think you boys could help with some of the bigger things. I want to flip all the mattresses. Vince, I was thinking about bringing in that kitchen hutch we found this summer. Sprucing it up and using it as a display for Kota's work." She turned toward me. "I think you need to focus on your website, social media, and getting more work created for your gallery and to sell. Also, organize your commission parameters and set up pricing. You're welcome to use the barn for any work—or my backroom, of course—but I know the garage at your place has a heater so your pallet and sled work may be best there." She wiped off a counter and hung the towel to dry.

I gawked at her.

"What?"

Shaking my head, I smirked. "I think I forgot that my grandma is a businesswoman in her own right. Commission parameters, pricing, social media—you just kinda have my head spinning."

She crossed her arms over her chest. "These are important parts to running your business."

"Oh, I know and I completely agree. I'm just loving the fact that *you* know all of it as well. Maybe you can be my business manager."

Mary Joy hooted. "Not a chance. I'll give orders and nag. I'll share your work far and near. But I've got my own damn business to run, so don't go thinking I'm doing your work for you."

"Noted," I said with a grin and gave her a hug. Between

my grandma being on my side and Vince being a new teammate I didn't even know I needed, Holly Hills really was starting to feel like the perfect place to settle in. At least for a while.

Mary Joy patted my back and went on. "Once the snow is clear, spend time in town. Maybe help Vince with some of his classes. The more people see you, the more interested they'll be when they hear about your artwork. I'll spread your cards around businesses—many have a community board where people stick their contact information. Your cards are very eye-catching and they'll definitely grab attention."

By the time Vince and I headed home, I had about a hundred new ideas and I wanted to get them all written down.

Yes, *home*. I felt at home in the sleepy little Christmas town I would have sworn I'd never in a million years want to *stay* in; it was a visit-only type place. Until Christmas magic got a hold of me.

What if you're just lulled into feeling content and safe in this little bubble and once you're outside of it, everything goes to hell?

I pushed away the thought.

"You gonna work or go straight to bed?" Vince asked as we stomped snow from our boots and removed our winter gear.

"I wanna make notes about some ideas I got earlier." I hopped up to sit on the chest freezer and spread my legs while yanking Vince close. When he smiled and wrapped his arms around my waist, I leaned in and nibbled at his ear. "But after that, I wasn't planning on sleeping just yet."

"You make your notes, I'll shower. While you're showering, I'll do my own note-making on some things that need done at the inn and how to schedule out some work I need to do around town once the snow is a bit more cleared." His words whispered over my lips, heating my body, sending anticipation coursing through me. "Meet me in about an hour?"

"In bed?"

Vince brushed a kiss over my lips before sucking my bottom lip between his teeth and pulling me close, my legs spread wide around his waist. "Don't be late."

An hour later, after scribbling notes in what I'd quickly deemed my idea notebook and rushing through a shower—as much as one can rush when knowing one's ass needs to be ready for plundering of one sort or another—I sauntered to the bedroom, towel around my waist.

The bed was empty.

My heart sank.

Then a warm chest pressed against my back and strong arms wrapped around my torso. "You looking for someone?"

I dropped my head back to Vince's shoulder. "Mmm," I hummed as his lips pressed open-mouthed kisses against my warm, sensitive skin. "Got a date. He told me not to be late, but it looks like *he* is."

"Rude. Gorgeous guy like you. If you were *my* date, I'd never leave you waiting." Vince's hands caressed up and down my torso, fingers flicking over my pebbled nipples. "What'dya say you just run off with me instead?"

I gasped as Vince's hand worked its way under the towel, cool air hitting my skin as the damp material fell to the floor and his hand wrapped around my stiff cock. "No can do. As hot as you seem, this guy I'm meeting has you beat. Dark eyes, dark hair, a little silver mixed in, sexy-as-hell scruff. Great personality to match."

Vince stroked me, thumbing through the pre-cum at my slit. "Does he know what to do with someone as beautiful as you?" The towel he was wearing dropped away and his hard dick pressed against my ass. "Know what to do with this pretty ass?"

I moved my arms above my head to grip the back of Vince's head and hold his mouth close to my skin as I moaned. "Mmm, yeah, he knows exactly what to do with me. Fucks me so good with his thick cock. Stretches me open and fills me with his cum." Vince's steely shaft pressed harder against my ass as one hand stroked me and the other hand plastered tight against my chest.

"He ever let you turn things around? Does he let you show what you can do with this throbbing cock?" Vince's words, muffled against my skin as I held his head, my arms still stretched high, turned my blood to lava.

"You know he does." I thrust my cock into Vince's fist. "He loves when I tongue his ass and work his tight muscle open. So good to see my hard cock sliding into his hot, greedy hole. He loves when I pump him full of my cum."

"Fuck, get on the bed now," Vince growled and pushed me toward the mattress, our fun little game over. "Ride me."

Lunging for the lube, I grabbed it and squirted some onto my hand. Slicking my ass first, I moved to straddle Vince and smear his cock as well. "We'll start like this, but then I want to be on my back."

"That can be arranged. Get on my dick."

Vince ran his hands up and down my thighs as I reached behind me to guide his cock to my entrance. My body protested as I slowly sank down his shaft, but the burning sting was brief as I adjusted to his thickness.

When I'd taken his full length, I paused and Vince stroked up my thighs, his hands ending up on my hips, his thumbs caressing my hip bones.

"You good? This okay?" he asked.

I nodded and raised my arms, tucking them behind my head, my torso stretched long and lean as I rode Vince's dick, my own leaking shaft bobbing in front of me as if begging for attention.

"Fuck, Kota," Vince growled, his legs shifting slightly as he dug his heels into the mattress. "So damn hot and tight, so fucking beautiful." He gripped my hips, not thrusting into me, just letting me set the pace and grind my ass on his shaft. "Touch yourself."

Loving that I was in a position of power—even with his dick in my ass, *I* was clearly running the show, Vince was just along for the ride—I ran my hands down to tease my nipples. With my bottom lip caught between my teeth, I watched Vince's dark eyes grow fiery when I pinched a nipple with one hand and took hold of my cock with the other.

"Mmmm, that's it, stroke that pretty cock," Vince murmured.

"Gonna need to flip over soon," I panted, feeling near orgasm already with his cock brushing that spot deep inside and my own hand coaxing my greedy dick along.

"Once I get you on your back, what do you want?" His words were gruff, as if he was enjoying our current position but already imagining our next.

"I want the best of both worlds." Spreading pre-cum around my sensitive cock head, I dropped my head back and rocked my hips. "Want you to wrap me in your arms, kiss me while you hold me close, and fuck me slow and hard until we both come."

With a groan, Vince caressed my thighs. "Your show, you call it when you're ready."

I loved that he was letting me make the call, but I knew from the twitch of his cock in my ass that he was more than ready to get me on my back. Whimpering as I lifted up and let his hard cock slide from my ass, flopping with a smacking sound against his stomach, I shifted to the mattress and spread my legs.

Vince applied a bit more lube before taking his place between my legs and pressing the head of his cock against my entrance. He slid in easily, pure pleasure coursing through me as he filled me again. When his balls pressed tightly against me, Vince paused with his arms wrapped under my shoulders, his mouth pressed to my neck as he breathed slowly and deeply.

"You okay?" I asked, wanting to trail my nails down his back and grip his ass, but knowing he needed a moment to compose himself.

"Just need a second or this is going to be over long before we want it to be."

"No biggie," I whispered in his ear, flicking my tongue over the lobe. "If you blow your load now, you can still get me off with your mouth while your cum drips from my hole."

"Fuck, Kota," Vince growled. "Not helping."

After another moment, he tightened his arms around me and settled into a slow rhythm of hard thrusts. Each time he slammed into me, I moaned into his mouth and deepened the kiss.

The friction of our bodies against my cock had my balls drawn tight and a tingle building at the base of my spine. "Fuck, Vince, I'm gonna come."

In answer, he increased the strength of his thrusts, but slowed the rhythm. "Do it, wanna feel you," he murmured against my lips.

My release shuddered through me as I shot hot, sticky ropes onto my belly, the mess quickly smeared between us as Vince continued to fuck into my body.

"So damn good, Kota. Love the way you feel on my cock when you come." His rhythm faltered and with a final thrust his cock throbbed in my ass as heat filled me.

After slow, sensual kisses, Vince slipped from my ass and reached for a towel. We wiped ourselves clean and quickly cuddled under the blankets.

As Vince's hand stroked my back and he pressed soft

kisses to my temple, I realized the warm feeling in my heart was an unfamiliar mix of love, contentment, happiness, and hope. Christmas was coming soon, I had a place to stay where I was loved and welcomed, I had a solid plan for making my passion for art work for me, and I had a man I could truly imagine spending every day for the rest of my life with.

Fuck the naysayers.

Love and Christmas magic were alive and well in Holly Hills.

TEN

VINCE

THE FIRST TWO years I lived in Holly Hills, Christmas was something that happened around me. I helped where needed and acknowledged the residents' happiness and excitement for the holiday, but I definitely kept to the perimeter and stayed as uninvolved as possible.

This year, while I definitely wasn't shouting Christmas greetings from rooftops, I was feeling a little more in the holiday spirit.

Christmas magic?

Settling in?

Getting older and realizing that what my parents had made Christmas for me didn't have to be my reality?

Kota?

Probably a healthy dose of all of those options.

Smiling as I heard Kota whistling in the kitchen as he made French toast, I thought about all the good of the last few weeks as the holiday approached.

First and foremost, Kota and I had grown closer with each passing day. We'd shared stories of our pasts—the good, the bad, and the ugly—and random facts about ourselves.

Even when the snow was cleared and we were able to be out and about town, Kota and I weren't usually far apart. We'd settled into a ridiculously easy routine of breakfast at home or in town, lunch at Mistletoe on Main or the Amaryllis with Mary Joy, and dinner was usually just the two of us back at home.

We were together so often, townsfolk would ask about the other if they saw us apart. In my past, that much togetherness would have sent me scrambling toward the hills, but with Kota, it was the easiest, most natural thing I'd ever done.

He'd joined me for several art classes and the students adored him. Partly because he was unbelievably engaging and partly because he brought a new flavor to our projects. I refused to let myself get too excited about it, but the thought of co-teaching art classes with Kota was definitely something I wanted if fate allowed it for my future.

Despite Mary Joy's almost-daily gentle suggestions that I tell Kota of my art critic side, I kept pushing it off. I'd gotten no responses to my inquiries so it likely didn't even matter. I'd turned down three requests to critique big-name pieces recently—the more I fell for Kota and settled myself in Holly Hills, the less I wanted to be associated with my former life, even if just from the periphery.

Kota's website was up and running. He had items for sale and had already sold a few pieces thanks to some of Mary Joy's friends seeing his information in her Facebook post. She'd also made sure his Twitter, Facebook, and Instagram were set up. Slowly, but surely, he was gaining followers. His TikTok account was actually growing faster than the rest and he posted a couple videos a day there, mostly of him drawing, working, creating.

We'd done a few fun TikTok videos of us working or playing, walking around town, eating lunch, random things, but those had gone to his personal social media and not his business accounts.

It felt good—strange, but good—that Kota wanted to show his friends what we had. Maybe we didn't know for sure where we were headed or what the future held for us, but I was sure as hell going to enjoy it while I could.

Kota had created several pieces for display and sale at the Amaryllis and many of them had been snatched up right away. A feeling of pride washed over me every time I saw Kota's eyes light up when another piece sold and bits of his future slotted into place—I'd known he was talented from the very first moment I'd seen his work and it felt good seeing it all slowly come to fruition.

The sleds had been a fun project we worked on together. In the end, we found ten sleds. We cleaned them all up and then kept one looking rustic and made one look brand new. Kota did his magic and depicted gorgeous winter scenes on both sleds, then we put them up on the website and social media for a vote. After a few days, the votes were pretty much tied, so we ended up doing five of the rustic vibe and five of the bright, shiny, new look.

Seven of the sleds sold to Holly Hills residents within a day.

The other three were gone over the weekend, snatched up by guests at the inn.

We needed new sleds for more projects.

The pallets were a huge hit. Seemed like every damn person in town, once the snow was cleared, had shown up at the Amaryllis—or seen pictures on social media—and fawned over the seasonal designs Kota had put on the pallets.

We'd dug around in the barn and pulled out every single pallet, but we definitely needed more. Kota and I planned a road trip after Christmas to deliver a few items and hit some places along the way in hopes of finding more sleds and pallet canvases for him to work on.

One of the biggest issues we'd run into was Kota always wanted to underprice his work. Mary Joy always overpriced it —proud grandmothers were allowed to. I was usually the intermediary and convinced him to price it at something fair, not too high, not too low. He'd balked at the price I insisted he put on the pallets and the sleds, but when they sold within a blink of an eye, he seemed to maybe realize his work was worth more than he was able to admit just yet.

"Hey, can you get the plates?" Kota asked as I came into the kitchen. "This is almost ready. And the bacon can come out of the oven."

I grabbed the plates and set the table before pulling the savory, crispy bacon from the oven. "Have you *seen* my plant?" I asked, unable to believe just how gorgeous and *alive* the Christmas cactus looked after the last couple weeks.

"You're welcome," Kota said as he smacked a kiss to my lips.

I grabbed him around the waist and pulled him in close for a long, lingering kiss, loving the taste of him on my tongue. Pulling away, getting a thrill at the beard-burn present on his jaw and neck from last night's—and this morning's—bedroom activities, I cocked a brow. "What am I thanking you for?"

"Well, aside from the awesome sex, I'm the main reason your plant didn't die a slow, torturous death."

I chuckled. "How do you figure?"

"If you hadn't rescued me from certain doom and brought me here, seduced me into your bed, and fallen head over heels for me, the plant would have been a goner."

"First, are you sure *I* seduced you? Second, I thought Christmas magic saved the plant?"

"Fine, we seduced each other. And Christmas magic had

to have *something* to work with. A.k.a., *me*. I was the special ingredient in making it all come together." He grinned and ran his fingers through the hair at the nape of my neck.

"*And* there's the awesome sex," I reminded him.

"Of course," he murmured against my lips, but then he frowned. "You know this is about more than just sex, right? Sex has always been easy and fun, but it's not like that with you."

"Gee, thanks," I deadpanned.

"No, that's not what I mean. Sex with you *is* easy and fun, but it's more than that. Ever since that first night, I've felt more with you than I've ever felt with anyone else."

"Same," I whispered, tipping his chin up for another kiss. It was on the tip of my tongue to tell him how much I loved him—now *that* had been a sucker punch to the gut when I realized it—but the timing didn't feel right. We'd jumped straight into sex and then a relationship, I wanted my declaration of love to come at the right time and not seem like I was saying it just because we'd done everything else at the speed of light.

We fell into a slow, lazy kiss filled with promise and hope.

When the timer buzzed on the oven, we pulled away slowly, our foreheads pressed together as we emerged from the blissful haze of contented happiness.

"Let's eat. I need to get some website work done, check emails, and get busy on some new pieces. I also want to put in an order for greeting cards, notepads, and stickers with that printing company." Kota pressed a kiss to my cheek. "What's on your agenda today?"

Kota had opted to use a printing company that catered to small businesses in need of printed materials. It wasn't a perfect solution, but it was workable for the time being.

"I need to head into town and fix a few things at the school. And Ivy asked me to come look at a pipe at the grocery." I filled my plate with French toast and slathered it with butter.

"How in the world did you get so handy with fixes and improvements?" Kota asked as he chomped on a piece of bacon.

I shrugged. "I watched a ton of YouTube videos the first few times someone asked me to fix something back when I was new in town. I still have to watch a few from time-to-time. I've always liked working with my hands and a lot of it just comes easy to me. Like, I see it in my head and I can work out what needs to be fixed or how to improve it. I think I'm mostly made for small odds-n-ends type jobs, nothing like remodeling an entire house, but I like what I do."

"Did you do similar work in your past?" Kota asked around a mouthful of battered bread and syrup.

"No," I said with a smirk. The opportunity was *right there*. I could have told him my art critic name—hell, maybe he wouldn't even recognize it. Honestly, I was being quite full of myself to assume he'd even know who I was. His artwork was nothing like the uppity, pretentious stuff I was used to critiquing.

But I was moving away from that.

There was no reason for him to know.

Is there a reason why he shouldn't *know?*

I thought about it while I ate. Kota and I were no longer just a fling. We maybe weren't a guaranteed forever, but I knew him well enough by now to know he wasn't with me for any reason other than he enjoyed what we had. He wasn't the type to use a person for personal gain.

So why was I so hesitant for him to know the Alan Vincent side of Vince Carter?

Because you've realized you very much don't like the person you were back then? Because you want to keep your present good *separated from your past bad and ugly?*

I'd already told Kota about my past, just not about who I was in the art world. Would he even care? Would it make an ounce of difference? If the situation was reversed, would I care if I found out Kota had been someone else in his past?

No.

Would I care if he hid it from me?

Wincing inwardly, I washed my food down with coffee.

Yeah, it would sting to find out he'd hidden something from me, even if he'd had good reason to.

Making up my mind to tell him about Alan Vincent, I stood and walked my empty plate to the sink. I didn't want to just blurt it out. Maybe with dinner? Over wine? Or wait until after the busyness of the holidays?

"Hey, leave the dishes, I'll do them later," Kota said as he stood. "I'm going to go do some office work before I work on pieces. See you at lunch?"

"Sounds good," I said, pulling him close for a kiss.

Love you I thought. But I didn't want to say the words until I'd cleared the secret hanging between us.

Kota headed off to his office work and I filled the sink with hot, soapy water. He'd said to leave the dishes, but I didn't mind doing them—especially since he cooked. That way, they'd be done when it was time to start dinner. Maybe I'd grab some steaks at Ivy's and see if Mary Joy had any extra side dishes I could serve with dinner. The grocery had a great little wine corner, I'd find a good red to complement the meal.

Thirty minutes later, as I puttered around the kitchen doing a bit of cleaning and straightening before heading into town, Kota came to the doorway with an odd look on his face.

"Hey, what's up?" I asked.

"What's your name?" he asked.

My heart sank. No way this was happening now, not the

moment I'd decided to come clean. My face must have shown guilt because Kota went on.

"Damn it, Vince. Or should I call you *Alan Vincent?*" He ran a hand over his face. "Why do I have an email from someone requesting to set up a Zoom meeting with me to discuss my work and possible avenues for selling because, and I quote, *I loved the work he sent, and if the great Alan Vincent thinks your work is good enough, I'm definitely interested in discussing it?*"

"I…" I paused, not sure how to go on.

"How did this person know who I was? How did they see my work?" Kota demanded.

I tossed a wet paper towel in the trash and sighed. "I sent pictures of your work to several of my old connections in the art world."

"You what?" Kota growled. "You sent unsolicited pictures of my work—without my permission? I don't even know where to start with all of this. The fact that you've been lying to me since the day we met or the fact that you basically stole my work or a huge fucked up combination of all of it."

"Let's sit down and talk about it," I suggested, gesturing toward the table.

"No," Kota bit out. "When I got the email—after spending way too long being dumbfounded by how in the hell *the great* Alan Vincent would have known anything about my work—I refused to fall victim to the usual clichéd misunderstanding and lack of communication. But now that I know you lied and stole my work, there's really no misunderstanding and there's no reason to talk about it." He stalked to the utility room and I followed as my heart plummeted.

"Where are you going?" I asked, my pathetic voice quivering on the verge of panicked tears.

"To Mary Joy's. I can't be here right now." He yanked on his coat and grabbed the keys to the ATV.

"Please, let me explain."

"I don't think I can listen to an explanation right now. I'm hurt and pissed." He whirled around as he reached the door. "You fucking *lied* to me and shared my work with people without my permission. I thought I knew who you are, but clearly I was very wrong." His face crumpled as tears threatened and he turned away and slammed out the door.

I sighed and brushed a tear from my cheek. "Fuck," I declared to the stark emptiness. Grabbing my phone as I saw the ATV drive past, I called Mary Joy.

"Good morning," she answered. "Are you boys coming for lunch?"

"He knows," I said as everything about the last several moments gathered in a brick in my gut.

"Oh dear," she sighed.

"He's coming to you. He's hurt and pissed. Says I lied to him and shared his work without permission."

"Is any of that inaccurate?" Mary Joy gouged at my pain.

Pinching the bridge of my nose, I groaned. "No. But please help me. Help him understand that none of it was to hurt him. I'd decided today that I was going to tell him about Alan Vincent tonight over wine and steaks. I figured since I hadn't heard from any of my inquiries, nothing was going to come of it. But I wanted to come clean and let him know who I used to be." I let my head fall back against the doorframe. "I have no idea who reached out to him or why they went directly to him—not sure *how* they knew to go to him." I winced. "I'm an idiot. Of course, they probably looked him up, found his site, used the contact information."

Mary Joy sighed. "Well, I see him pulling up now. I'm not sure how much I can defend what you did—I'm not going to say I told you so—but I *will* try to make sure he sees that you'd never try to hurt him. Maybe focus on the fact that someone is interested in his art."

My voice caught in my throat and I cleared it before continuing. "I love him," I said, my words raw and rough.

"Well, that explains the stupidity. Don't expect him home tonight." She ended the call.

I wandered into the kitchen, my heart aching, and did my best to gather myself together. Kota had been insistent he not be cliché by letting a misunderstanding and miscommunication come between us, but he'd not been able to avoid the storming off to lick his wounds storyline.

And what will you do? Go wallow in your misery or buck up and get on with it?

As much as my heart wanted to scream, cry, and wallow, I knew no good would come from it. I had work to do and, if Kota was never able to forgive me for what I'd done—even if it came from good intentions—then I had to figure out how to move on without him.

If Kota needed some time away from me—no matter how badly that hurt—then I'd give it to him and hope he was eventually able to come back so we could talk things out. Hopefully, Mary Joy could help him see beyond his hurt and anger. Despite my heartache, I couldn't help but wonder who had reached out to Kota and what opportunities they might have for him.

I grabbed my coat and phone and dragged my sorry ass to my truck. It was going to be a long-ass day.

ELEVEN
KOTA

I KNOCKED snow from my boots and took them off on Grandma's back porch before shedding my coat and gloves. My eyes stung from the cold and tears and my heart hurt, but neither compared to the raw anger and humiliation simmering inside.

When I'd opened the email, it had taken several minutes of reading and re-reading it to finally piece together some sort of answer as to what the hell was going on.

Alan Vincent was a name I recognized, but not one I was overly familiar with. When I Googled the name, I was floored to see Vince, *my Vince*, staring back at me from the images— but a different person altogether as well; Alan Vincent appeared polished, high-society, aloof...nothing like the Vince I'd met and fallen in love with.

And yeah, wasn't *that* just a punch to the gut? I'd never been in love—I'd *thought* I loved others, but nothing had ever been like what I had with Vince.

And then I find out he wasn't who he said he was.

Or more accurately, he's Vince, but he never told me about who he used to be.

Article after article mentioned him in correlation with huge names in the art world. I clicked on several of his critiques, flabbergasted by the prestigious pieces he'd been invited to offer his opinion on.

Then I found the articles about Cecil and the accusations against Vince and the company he worked for. I knew the story, but even if I hadn't, I had a hard time understanding why blame was leveled so much at Vince when Cecil appeared to have been the one who took advantage of the situation. He got butthurt when Alan Vincent didn't praise his work, but that didn't mean Vince had done anything wrong.

After those articles, I skimmed the pieces that spoke of how Alan Vincent had all but fallen off the face of the earth and only did critiques from time-to-time these days. No one knew where he was living, he didn't do interviews, and he only wrote for a few top-notch art publications.

Holy fuck.

I was sleeping with someone famous and he'd never once told me. And it wasn't like it didn't come up, he had several opportunities to tell me.

I ran my hand through my hair as I walked into Mary Joy's kitchen.

Finding out he'd lied to me was hard. Realizing he'd shared my work without my permission was a kick to the nuts I'd never seen coming. My gut reaction had been to pack up and leave once Vince had left, but I refused to play the part of the character in the cheesy holiday movie who blows a situation out of proportion. Instead, I'd confirmed my worst fears with Vince before leaving. There had been no misunderstanding. And the only lack of communication had been on his part.

My head ached from crying and gritting my teeth against the anger.

"Have some hot chocolate. Sit down," Mary Joy said. "Let's have a chat. I'm guessing you've got a lot to unload."

I took the steaming mug and sat down, but her words clicked and I tensed. "Wait, you *knew* he was lying to me? You *knew* and didn't tell me? You fucking encouraged me to fall in love with a liar and a thief?"

Mary Joy sat across from me and leaned in on her elbows. "Kota Christopher, you have every right to be upset and I'll gladly let you vent, but I will *not* tolerate disrespect or profanity in my place of business."

I took a deep breath. "I'm sorry. I just don't understand how you could have *known* and let me humiliate myself."

"What in the world are you talking about? First, yes, I knew. I found out by mistake and promised I wouldn't tell. It was never my secret to divulge. He's Vince Carter now—he's been Vince Carter since the day he came here. I don't know this Alan Vincent person, but I get the feeling Vince doesn't like that part of his life very much. If Holly Hills was what he needed to start over and be a person he could *like*, then that's what I want him to have. There was no danger to you not knowing he was a high-society art critic long before he met you." She folded her hands. "Now, what is this poppycock about humiliating yourself?"

I flung my hand in the air. "You said it yourself. He's used to high-society. Have you *seen* the art he worked with? And here I am pretending that my pathetic drawings on sleds and pallets, *greeting cards* for..." I paused before cursing. "He must think I'm such a loser trying to sell my work when the most it should ever be is a hobby."

Mary Joy folded her arms over her chest. "Are you quite finished?"

Frowning at her over my mug, I sipped my hot chocolate before continuing. "For now, but don't even get me started on the fact he basically stole my work and shared it without my permission."

"I'm not defending his choice to hide his past from you. I encouraged him to tell you from the moment I realized there was something between the two of you. However, and I'm sure you know this story, Vince was hurt by someone who used him for his name."

"Something *I* would never do," I interjected.

"I know that. And Vince knows that now. That man has wanted nothing but the best for you since the moment he drove your scrawny ass up the hill. He's worked his butt off right along with you to give you every opportunity and success—he's like a proud parent every time a piece of your work sells. Did he screw up in not telling you about his past? Yes, but he also had the right to want to keep that part of him buried." Mary Joy took a sip from her coffee.

"It would be one thing if his past was completely unrelated, but he's an art critic—a huge name one—and I'm a struggling artist. It makes me look...I don't know... desperate? Pathetic? Like I can only get interest in my art because of his name?" I pinched the bridge of my nose. "How am I supposed to know if offers that come my way are *real* or because the great Alan Vincent called in a favor?"

Mary Joy patted my hand. "Well, that's something you'll need to discuss with Vince, but I'd venture a guess that those individuals who may want to discuss your art and your options are only going to be interested in work they think will sell. They aren't going to go out on a limb for someone— even if he's the boyfriend of a great former art critic— without a pretty good idea their risk will be worth it."

That made sense—as much as I wanted to keep wallowing in my anger, Grandma was doing a damn good job of talking me down—but it still hurt that he hadn't trusted me enough to tell me who he was in his past life. We'd told each other so much, why had he felt the need to keep that piece from me?

He told you everything about his past except his name and profession. He told you about the Cecil mess. Would his name or profession change the way you feel about him?

Gripping at my anger, I flattened my palm against the table. "That doesn't change that he shared my work without my permission."

"True." Mary Joy cocked her head to the side. "May I offer a different perspective?"

I shrugged like a petulant child, knowing she was going to share her thoughts whether I liked it or not.

"He shared your work with people he knew in hopes of getting your business off the ground. Is that really any different than me sharing your work on Facebook, Twitter, Instagram? I've shared as your grandmother, but I've also shared from my business accounts. Is it any different than you posting your work on social media and people adding it to their stories or clicking the share button?" She raised an eyebrow and waited.

"He could have told me about it," I mumbled.

"He could have—probably should have—but I think he wanted to avoid getting your hopes up in case nothing came from it." She patted my hand. "Vince is a fine man and he's crazy about you—don't think I missed what you said about falling in love with him—but he's just a man. He makes mistakes the same as the rest of us do." She wagged a finger in my direction. "Let's not forget that you only came to visit me because you thought I was dying. We *all* make mistakes. We own them, learn from them, and move on."

"I just wish he would have talked to me. We've talked about so much, it hurts that he hid things from me."

"I hear what you're saying and you two need to discuss

that." She finished her coffee and took our mugs to the sink. "Did you respond to the person who emailed you?"

I bristled. "I don't want an opportunity handed to me, I want to work for it."

Mary Joy crossed her arms. "Stuff and nonsense. If it's okay for *me* to share your work and display it and help, that's no different than Vince doing the same. Talk to him, look into the possible opportunities." When I was stubbornly quiet, she continued. "There's a *reason* you came here, a reason you met Vince. Maybe things have gotten a little messy and uncertain, but don't let hurt feelings and anger run your life and make your decisions for you."

I nodded. "Can I stay over tonight? I need to do some work and clear my head."

"Of course. As long as you promise to discuss things with Vince tomorrow. We have Christmas in a few days and I don't want there to be bad feelings between you."

By the time I crashed into bed that night, my heart was no longer in shreds and my anger had subsided. I was battered and bruised, but I was man enough to admit that—despite my wish to not fall prey to a cliché—I'd let hurt and anger get the best of me. I was ready to have a civil conversation with Vince.

He was truly the best thing that had ever happened to me. Whether he was connected to the art world or not, I'd still be head over heels in love with him and want to spend time with him. As much as it humbled me to know my work would never be what he was used to critiquing, I wanted him on my side, cheering me on.

Even if Vince wanted to continue critiquing as Alan Vincent, I wanted him in my life and supporting me. I was ready to work through whatever challenges our separate lives might bring as long as it meant we could continue in our shared life together.

What if this person who contacted you gives you an amazing opportunity but it would require you to leave Holly Hills? Leave Vince and Mary Joy?

My heart froze.

No use borrowing trouble. I'd talk things out with Vince, contact this Martin guy who'd emailed me, and we'd go from there. We had Christmas with family and friends to celebrate before any big decisions needed to be made.

The next morning, I pulled the ATV into the garage and found Vince under my car. When the snow had cleared enough, he'd driven me down the hill to rescue my vehicle. He'd been saying he wanted to check the oil and fluids, make sure the tire pressure was correct, give it a good once-over.

By the looks of him sprawled under the car, Vince had taken to staying busy just as I had.

He slid out from underneath the front of the car and sat up, wiping his hands on a rag. "Morning," he said, clearly apprehensive and wondering how this was going to play out.

"Morning. Any chance we could talk?" I hung the ATV keys on the hook. "I'll make you a coffee."

Hope shone in his eyes and I hated that I'd made him worry.

I also hated that he'd caused the situation, but that didn't mean I wanted him upset.

"I'll be in in about ten minutes. Let me finish this so it's drivable."

I headed inside, wanting desperately to work through the tension between us. We'd fallen in with each other so fast, so easily, our first rough spot was kinda shocking. Of course, our first rough spot was also quite a doozy. If we could get through something like this, we could face anything.

Even if you have to move away?

I really didn't want to think about it.

I placed a steaming mug of coffee on the table just as Vince came through the door. I stood at the counter and sipped my hot chocolate as he stomped snow from his boots and unzipped his coat.

He washed his hands at the sink and dried them quickly before turning to me and tentatively reaching for my waist. With a soft sigh, I took a step toward him and let him wrap me in his arms as I held him tightly.

"Kota, I'm so damn sorry. I *never* meant to hurt you." His gruff whisper sent shivers through me.

"I know. I shouldn't have run off, but I needed a little perspective and time to clear my head."

"Are we okay? I can spend a few nights at the inn if you need more time. I can…"

I threaded my fingers through the hair at the back of his head and pulled him down for a slow, gentle kiss. "We need to talk, but we're fine. I'm sorry for running off and not being willing to communicate. We both made mistakes, but you're wrong if you think one mess up is going to make me give up the best thing that's ever happened to me."

"We *do* have to think of the plant as well, this relationship isn't just about us." Vince kissed the tip of my nose when I laughed. "Coffee smells good."

We settled at the table.

I took a deep breath. "The two things that hurt me the most were that you didn't tell me about Alan Vincent and you shared my work without my knowledge."

Vince took my hand, his thumb caressing my skin as he spoke. "In the beginning, I didn't want you knowing about Alan Vincent because I'd been taken advantage of once when someone used me for my name. But then I got to know you and realized you'd never do that. But we had this amazing thing going and I didn't want to ruin it by bringing my past into it. I told myself I'd told you about the Cecil mess and that was enough." He paused to sip his coffee. "I didn't like myself very much back when I was Alan Vincent. Sure, I made tons of money, had a lot of power and prestige—at least in the art world—and could have sex with anyone I wanted if I opted to. But I wasn't happy, not truly. When the shit with Cecil went down, I left, thinking my life was over. But I found this little place, left Alan Vincent behind, and became Vince Carter—slowly, but surely, my life transformed into something resembling contentment and happiness. Yeah, I'm able to live this way now because Mary Joy lets me stay rent free and Alan Vincent made me a ton of money I've squirreled away—and yes, I've still been doing a few critiques a year to pad my savings—but this place, these people, the changes I made when I came here, I needed it all. I didn't want to dirty what we had by telling you about someone I didn't even like."

I gave his hand a squeeze. "I can understand and respect that. I guess I'm just hurt that you thought I'd ever use you or care about who you were in the past. I like Vince Carter, not Alan Vincent. I think it just kinda feels like you didn't trust me."

"I can see that. Please know that I trust you more than anyone I've ever known. No one aside from Mary Joy knows about Cecil, and you know a lot more about it than she does. I'm embarrassed by the person Alan Vincent was—even though the art world would deem him this amazing person, I know who he really was and I don't ever want to be him again."

I took a drink of my hot chocolate. "Why did you share my work without asking me?" I held up my hand. "And let me just say, I realize it's not *all* that different from Mary Joy sharing my stuff or random people sharing on social media. But this felt like you deliberately went behind my back."

"You went to the bathroom and I got this crazy idea that I could do something good with my old life's connections. It ended up being something I wanted to surprise you with if it worked out and something I didn't want to get your hopes up with if it didn't. I *did* sneak screen shots of your work and I think I realized even right then that I shouldn't have done it without your knowledge, but I want so much for you—all of the opportunities and for your business to be a success," he paused, glanced at me, and looked away, "and for you to have a reason to stay here. I wasn't thinking and I'm sorry. Your work is so damn good, I just got excited."

"My work is *nothing* compared to the pieces you're used to critiquing."

"You're right, I never would have deemed your work as *art* back in my Alan Vincent days," Vince said.

Ouch. I winced.

"Hear me out. That wasn't meant as a put-down. You've likely seen the art I've worked with. Much of it is amazing, some of it is ridiculous, all of it brought joy to the creator or the observer or both at some point." Vince squeezed my hand. "But none of it spoke to me. You have the same talent as all of those artists even though your creations are vastly different. It's not skill or talent in question. You've got amazing nature scenes, gorgeous animals, cute cartoons, eye-catching geometric designs—most of which would be looked down on by the snobs in my past, but your work is heartfelt. It's real and meaningful, it brings people happiness. Not to mention, *real* people can afford your work. The stuff I worked with sold for hundreds of thousands of dollars—most of it wasn't purchased because it spoke to the buyer but because they want to brag about it. People are so happy to decorate their homes with your pieces. They want those cute little greeting cards to send to friends." He took a deep breath. "The work in my past never brought me happiness, but seeing you work, seeing people happily buy your pieces, seeing your art be sought after by normal, everyday people? I'd rather see that every single day than critique another piece of boring, shallow, snobby artwork."

"What if it was exciting, deep, and genuine artwork?"

Vince smirked. "Even then, I'd rather be here doing this, watching you, being *real* with you."

"What if I can't have my dream and stay here?"

A frown flitted over Vince's face, but he schooled his features quickly. "I've fallen in love with you and I want you in my life, but if I had to give it all up for you to find opportunities and success, I'd do it. I love you and want the best for you, even if that means I have to let you go."

My heart was in my throat. *I love you, too.* God, I did. So much. But the time didn't feel right to say it. We still had decisions to make. If I had to leave and he wouldn't come with me, maybe it was for the best that I never admitted I loved him.

I cleared my throat and sniffed. "Maybe I don't want to be given up." I picked up my phone. "Will you call Martin with me?"

"Martin Englebert?" Vince's eyes went wide. "That's who emailed you?"

I nodded.

"He was my top hope. He isn't someone who would directly do anything with your art, but he has a ton of connections. Let's call him and see what he has to say."

An entire hour later, after the Vince and I spoke with a very kind and enthusiastic Martin, I ended the call. Martin had asked a ton of questions about what I wanted to do with my work, where I wanted to see it, if I wanted to stay independent or go commercial, and on and on and on.

My head was reeling by the time we finished the call.

Something Martin had said ran on a loop in my head. *"Son, far be it from me to tell the artist where to find inspiration and work. I always like to be near the epicenter of the action. If you're like me, you might want to consider moving closer to where you can keep an eye on things, be right in the thick of it. But if you've found a place where your artistic heart is happy and productive, don't give it up. We can make things happen anywhere these days."*

That night, as we got ready for bed, I asked the question that had been weighing on me. "If I felt like I needed to be somewhere else in order to keep creating and making my dreams come true, would you go with me?"

Vince was quiet for a moment and the silence killed me. "I don't know. Maybe me staying here and letting you spread your wings out there is what I have to do. Maybe it's my part in the love and Christmas magic."

"How is letting me go, giving up on us, part of the magic of Christmas?" I asked, hurt and sadness tingeing my words.

"Just like you were the special ingredient in Christmas magic bringing back my plant and showing me what happiness is, maybe I'm the special ingredient in the recipe for your future success." Vince wrapped his arms around me and kissed the top of my head.

"A future without you?" I honestly didn't see how I could focus on my dreams without Vince. Until Holly Hills, I'd never known he was part of what I longed for. But now that I'd fallen in love with him, I didn't think I could create and be happy if he wasn't by my side. It hurt to think I maybe wasn't enough reason for him to consider moving.

Is it fair of you to expect him to do that? He's finally found happiness in this little town. How can you ask him to move just to keep you happy?

"A future without you sounds like a nightmare, but I don't know that I can answer your question just yet. Let's get through Christmas and see where we are then." Vince tipped my chin up and brushed a kiss over my lips. "No matter what, I love you and want you to know how very special you are to me. You're the best thing that's ever happened in my life. I don't *want* to say goodbye."

"Then don't."

"If you moving away is best for you and me staying here is best for me, I don't know how we work around that. Let's sleep on it. Christmas is just a day away, let's not make any decisions just yet."

I love you. Please don't let this be the end of us.

We'd started out as just a holiday fling, but we'd found so much more together. I wasn't ready to let him go.

Then stay in Holly Hills. You can create your art from anywhere.

It was true, I could. I think I mostly just wanted to know that Vince would move with me if that's what I wanted. Which was unfair and immature, I knew that. I had a lot of thinking to do before Christmas.

Shit, I also needed a gift for Vince.

As my eyes grew heavy, I recalled all of the amazing moments we'd had together—even just the day-to-day mundane things—and slowly an idea grew in my head.

TWELVE
VINCE

CHRISTMAS EVE DAWNED sunny and almost warm. The weatherman predicted the warmth of Christmas Eve would be partly responsible for the huge amount of snow expected on Christmas Day. A greedy part of my heart thrilled at the thought of more snow falling and keeping Kota with me for at least a little longer.

After my screw-up and our subsequent sit-down, Kota and I had clung to each other as if we were spending our last days together. And maybe we were. Our wake-up sex that morning had quickly morphed into lovemaking and I never wanted to lose what we had.

But could I leave Holly Hills?

You left the city and your past to start over. You can do anything you damn well please.

But I *liked* who I'd become in Holly Hills. I liked the slow, easy days, the friendships, my little art classes, the life I'd built for myself.

Will you like all of that as much when you're lonely and missing Kota?

Part of me felt like it would be best to wish Kota all the

best and close the book on this brief chapter of my life. Maybe meeting him had been the catalyst for me to realize I was capable of love. Having Kota in my life had shown me that Christmas wasn't all that bad. Hell, I even broke down and accepted there was *something* to the whole love and Christmas magic. Perhaps that was the *why* of Kota coming to town and I needed to stop trying to make it more.

But the other part of me—the part that felt *very* strongly and was screaming at me to get my head out of my ass and do what my heart was begging me to do—said that Kota and I met for a reason and it wasn't meant to be a brief, fleeting encounter that we looked back on fondly. There was *no way* two people were as connected and insanely good together as we were in such a short amount of time without there being something else at play. Kota and I were meant to meet, meant to fall in love, meant to be together. Christmas magic and my gorgeous plant be damned, even without those things in the mix, there was no way to deny Kota and I were meant to be.

When you loved someone, you wanted the best for them. If that meant Kota needed to move somewhere and only visit Holly Hills, then so be it. I'd move with him and we'd visit Holly Hills as often as possible. I could teach art anywhere. I could do handyman work anywhere.

But I couldn't imagine my life without Kota by my side.

What if you leave Holly Hills and the magic between you disappears? Maybe it's just this place that has you both so gaga for each other.

I scoffed. Love and Christmas magic were alive and well in the tiny town, but what I felt for Kota was more than just the magic of a small Christmas town. I knew that without a shadow of a doubt.

Kota spent the entire day locked away working on a secret project while I racked my brain thinking of what I could give him for Christmas. I'd always tried to stay away from all things Christmas, but now I wanted more than anything to show Kota what he meant to me with a gift. But it had to be just right.

That night, after slow, easy kisses led to hot, frenzied frotting, I wrapped Kota in my arms and kissed the top of his head. Holding him, thinking about everything I knew about the man I loved, I realized Kota didn't need material gifts. I had the perfect idea and couldn't wait to give it to him the next day.

I woke to a wet heat engulfing my morning erection and nearly came on the spot. "Fuck, Kota, don't get me wrong, I love this type of wake-up call," I panted as he swirled his tongue around my head before swallowing me deep. "But damn it, keep that up and I'll blow before we get to anything else."

Kota popped off my cock and crawled up my body to plaster himself to my chest and kiss me with warm, wet lips. "Want you in me. Wanna feel you come in me. Then I want you to finger fuck me—keep all your cum from dripping out —while you suck me off."

"Fuck," I growled against his mouth. "Roll over."

Kota shifted off me and onto his back, spreading his legs as he reached for his ass and slipped a finger inside. "I already stretched and lubed. Get in me," he demanded.

After slicking myself from the bottle on the bedside table, I settled between Kota's legs and pressed the head of my cock against his tight, hot entrance. Between the blow job and the image Kota had painted for me, there was no way I'd last long once his body took me in.

He gasped and moaned as my dick sank into him. Even with prepping, Kota's tight ring of muscle fought against my intrusion. When his body finally relaxed enough to let me in, I groaned when my balls pressed against his skin.

"You good?"

Kota hummed, his legs coming around my waist. "So good. I don't care how you do it, just want to feel you come inside. Don't wait for me. Want your mouth on my cock and your fingers pumping your cum in my ass before I come."

Just his words had my slow, easy thrusts faltering and my balls drawing up tight. "Fuck, Kota." With my eyes fixed on his, I pumped my hips harder and faster knowing my orgasm was only seconds away. Imagining the fantasy Kota asked for, I growled as my release rolled through me, my hot load shooting deep into his ass.

With a final pulse of my spent cock, I slipped from his body with a slow, sensual kiss on his lips. Pressing kisses down his chest, nipping at his taut nipples, flicking my tongue over his naval, I reached my destination and licked the slit of his leaking cock. Cupping his balls and teasing a finger over his taint first, I slowly moved my fingers to his hole. Evidence of my orgasm slicked his pucker and I easily slipped in two fingers as I sucked his cock to the back of my throat.

"Fuuuck," Kota moaned. "Yessss." His tight, hot ass clenched around my fingers as I savored his pre-cum on my tongue. "Oh fuck, so good. Next time, you rim me with your cum dripping from my ass while you jack me off."

My cock jerked in response to that suggestion and I hummed around his shaft, sending a shudder through him. Slipping my fingers in and out, slick with lube and cum, I ran a thumb over the seam of his tight sac. He was close. I continued sucking his cock as my fingers dipped deep to brush over his prostate.

Kota's hips bucked but I put an arm over him to hold him in place. Licking and sucking, loving the taste of him on my tongue, I finger fucked my cum back into his body as I teased over his bundle of nerves.

His babbling whimpers and grunts grew more and more desperate as he fisted the sheets with one hand and my hair in the other. "Fuck, Vince, gonna come." His cock exploded on my tongue in hot, salty bitterness and I let him ride out his orgasm as his tight ring of muscle clenched around my slick fingers.

Pulling my fingers from his ass and letting his cock slip from between my lips, I moved up his body and drew him into a long, deep kiss. Our languid tongues moved together slowly, savoring the flavor and the easy contact that was now as essential as breathing.

"Merry Christmas," I whispered at Kota's ear before pressing a kiss against his temple.

"From the man who doesn't like Christmas? The self-proclaimed Christmas grump?" Kota's eyes sparkled as he cupped the sides of my face and smiled up at me.

"Someone showed me it's not that bad. Plus, I love you. If you love Christmas, it's bound to rub off on me as well." I kissed him again, my heart only slightly hurt that Kota had yet to say he loved me, too.

"It's a Christmas miracle." He smacked my ass and kissed me with a grin. "Let's get cleaned up. I want to fix breakfast and then spend the whole morning in front of the fire watching movies."

"We're going to Mary Joy's, right?" I rolled from bed and stretched.

"Yeah, but not until afternoon. I guess she's doing a big to-do with the guests who opted to take part. We'll have an early dinner at the inn with her later." Kota got out of bed. "Separate showers or we'll never get breakfast. Plus, I have a gift I want to give you."

After showers, I met Kota in the kitchen and gratefully

took the steaming mug of coffee he handed to me. "You realize it's only like six a.m., right? We could have slept longer."

"We *could* have, but then you wouldn't have gotten to blow your load in my ass and finger fuck me while sucking me off." He pressed himself against me, knowing his words would turn me on. "Plus, we've got all day to be lazy. I'm calling for a nine a.m. nap. Maybe even a one o'clock snooze before we head over to Grandma's." He grinned as he wrapped his arms around my neck. "Now, pancakes, waffles, French toast, or something else?"

"Let's do waffles this time." My heart lurched as I thought about Kota and I building Christmas traditions. Would this be the one and only holiday we'd have together? Or was this the start of many more to come? We really needed to talk, but maybe Christmas Day wasn't the time or place. I'd decided I'd go wherever he asked me to go, so I just needed to get it out of my head that traditions had to be *here* in Holly Hills. We could create our own memories from anywhere, as long as we were together.

"Perfect. Can you do the eggs and bacon while I start the batter?" Kota grabbed the recipe book. "And turn on some Christmas music. The fireplace channel should be on. Let's set the mood." He winked.

We settled into a fun and easy breakfast-making event with lots of laughter, kisses, and love.

There was no way I could ever give this man up.

"Time for gifts!" Kota slapped a hand against my thigh as our second Christmas movie of the day wrapped up. "Gifts first. Then maybe sex before a nap."

"Maybe?"

He winked. "Depends. My gift may overwhelm you so much that you're forced to ravish me."

"Or you'll remember that I'm rapidly approaching my senior years and have mercy on my poor dick," I teased. We laughed about my age affecting my sex drive, but honestly, I'd never felt more alive and energetic since meeting Kota. Happiness and contentment could do that to a person.

He pulled me up from the pile of blankets we were still using as a couch in the living room. "Who said your dick has to do any work? Maybe I just want you to spread yourself open and let me go to town on my very favorite ass." Our teeth clicked together as we laughed and kissed, slowly morphing into a warm embrace that I hoped conveyed to Kota just how much he meant to me.

"I get to go first." He maneuvered me to the wide arch between the living room and the kitchen. "Don't move." Kota grabbed a flat, square item wrapped in brightly colored red, green, and silver. "I'm hoping most of this doesn't need explaining. Open it."

I tore open the paper and Kota laughed.

"What?" I raised a brow.

"I don't know, I guess I pegged you for an open gently, save the wrapping paper type guy."

I chuckled. "If you're done critiquing my gift-opening skills, may I go on?"

Kota gestured for me to continue.

When the paper was torn away, I was left holding a ten by ten canvas divided into nine square sections. In the top left square were our names, the year, and *Holly Hills*.

My eyes, already stinging from threatening tears, traveled to the middle of the top row. A perfect replica of Kota's car, stuck in a ditch, snow all around, the very edge of a truck bumper and a man who looked suspiciously like me.

The top right picture was a snow scene. Pristine, white, beautiful.

The middle right side showed a perfectly drawn image of the blankets in the living room. I couldn't help but chuckle. I wondered when Mary Joy was planning to return the couch.

This canvas depicted our beginning. Kota was telling our story through his art.

Smack dab in the middle was the spectacular Christmas cactus in all of its blooming glory. Truly, I wasn't sure I'd ever seen a more gorgeous plant and it was even more impressive to know the near-death it was resurrected from. That plant had been part of Kota and me from the beginning. I loved that he put it in the very middle.

The middle row, far left was the happiest, fullest, most perfect Christmas tree I'd ever seen. He'd gotten even the most minute details of tinsel into the drawing.

My heart clenched slightly on the bottom left corner when I saw the dreary winter scene. I knew this was Kota's depiction of our argument—a visual representation of the emotions we'd both experienced and a reminder to keep the truth first and foremost.

The twin sleds in the bottom middle made me smile—one brand new and shiny, the other old and rustic, but both beautiful with their very own tiny winter scene painted on them. The sleds weren't something I would have thought of including in our story, but leave it to Kota to find meaning where others wouldn't. The sleds represented him and me. They were the start of something good with his art business. We grew to know and love each other as we prepared those sleds in the barn. The two sleds were different, but they complemented each other perfectly and I loved that Kota had included them in our story.

The bottom right picture was a couple, kissing under mistletoe. "What's this one?"

Kota took the canvas from me, placed it to the side, and pointed up.

Above us, hanging from the archway, was a bundle of mistletoe.

He took my face in his hands. "I want to build a home with you, want to make memories. I want us to travel around looking for pallets and sleds and inspiration. Every damn year, I want to freeze our asses off as we go find the perfect tree. I want to kiss you under the mistletoe for as long as you'll have me."

With my heart in my throat and tears glistening, I pulled him close and pressed my forehead against his. "And if I want you for as many Christmases as we're blessed to celebrate from here until the end of time?"

Kota sniffed and grinned, a tear slipping down his cheek. "Then I guess we better make sure our mistletoe supply is solid."

I crushed our mouths together, kissing him with every ounce of love in my heart.

Kota broke the kiss. "In case it wasn't evident in the pictures and the fact that I basically just invited myself to move in with you permanently, I love you." He pressed a kiss to my lips. "I love you."

"I love you, too." Our kisses were slow and easy, holding such promise and hope.

"I'm sorry I waited to tell you. I've wanted to for a while, but the timing never felt right. But don't ever think that I don't love you with all of my heart." Kota tucked his head under my chin and sighed into me as I held him close.

"You want your gift?"

His head popped up, his eyes wide. "A Christmas gift from the man who hates Christmas?"

I chuckled. "I told you, *someone* may have helped to convince me that the holiday isn't all that bad." I pulled him to the blankets and we settled in, Kota on my lap, my arm around his shoulder as I held his hand. "Aside from art supplies, I didn't know what type of material items I could get you, so I went a different direction."

Kota gave me a soft smile. "Anything you put thought into giving me will be amazing, I already know. Just the fact that you want to give me something on a holiday you aren't crazy about means a lot."

"So, the first thing is maybe as much for me as it is for you."

His eyebrow crooked up.

"And I didn't do it just for you, but it's something I want you to be aware of from the very beginning. No more secrets." I swallowed thickly, knowing I was making the right decision, but apprehensive all the same. "I've continued critiquing as opportunities came along because it allowed me to bring in an income and save for the future." I laughed as I caressed his thumb. "As hard as it is to believe, I'm not raking in the big bucks doing handyman work and teaching art classes."

Kota grinned.

"I'm committed to writing four critiques for the highest paying publication this year, but after that, I'm done."

"What? No, why?" Kota frowned.

"Alan Vincent is no longer who I am. I should have said goodbye to him two years ago when I came here. I haven't gotten joy in working as him for a very long time and it's time to say goodbye. I'm happy as Vince Carter. I've submitted a final article for publication after the fourth critique of the year is published. It's a goodbye to that part of my life."

Kota leaned in and kissed my cheek. "As long as you're happy. If you want to continue writing as Alan Vincent, I support you one hundred percent. If leaving him behind is what feels right, I stand beside you for that, too."

"Thank you. Leaving him in the past is what my heart says to do." I cleared my throat. "The next part of my gift to you is also a bit more for me than you." I frowned and chuckled. "Damn, wasn't thinking this all the way through. Gifts for *you* shouldn't end up being more for me."

Kota smirked. "Seeing you happy and moving on from the past is gift enough for me."

"Well, I wanted to say thank you for helping me see that Christmas isn't as bad as I'd convinced myself. My parents made things miserable for me so it made sense that I'd associate those bad feelings they always stirred up at Christmas—a holiday that led them to laying the nastiest of their comments on thick. But you've shown me that Christmas doesn't have to be about that negativity. Watching you celebrate, seeing happiness and excitement glowing in your eyes, I've realized that I want to take this special time of the year and build new, positive memories around it."

Kota's eyes sparkled. "Love and Christmas magic finally wore you down."

I snorted. "That's part of it. I can't say I'm a firm believer, but there's no doubt something to it. But more than that, I believe in *us* and what love can do when the right two people find each other."

"Have I told you lately that I adore you?" Kota pressed a kiss to my lips. "When we met, I told myself that I *would* get you to like Christmas. The fact that you not only see the good of the holiday, but also want to continue building on that with me? That's the most perfect gift in the world."

"Before I tell you what your actual gift is, I want you to know that I'm willing to move wherever you need to be to make your business a success." I cupped Kota's face and pressed a kiss to his lips as he gaped in stunned silence. "I can work from anywhere. I'll find odds and ends to do, offer art classes, hell, I'll even do freelance writing under a new name if needed. We can talk about your plan, but don't ever think that I'd be able to let you go. It's just not something I can do."

He smiled. "That means the world to me and I appreciate it so much. But, while we're on the subject, I need *you* to know that I've decided—at least for the near future—to work from Holly Hills. You're here, my grandma is here. We can travel as needed for work, but I'm not ready to leave here."

I kissed him hard. "That's the perfect lead-in to my gift. We're going to take Mary Joy's RV and go on a month-long road trip."

Kota's eyes went wide.

"In April, so we're hopefully done with the majority of the snow, we'll pack up and hit the road. That gives us time to map out the best places to hunt for old sleds and pallets. You'll bring your supplies and work whenever inspiration strikes. We'll document the trip on your social media and hopefully grow your following." I eyed him carefully, hoping he liked the idea.

"I love it. It sounds so perfect. If it goes well, maybe we make it a continuing thing. Spring trip, summer trip, fall trip, and then we spend winter holed up here at home." Kota wiggled with excitement.

"Do you know how much I love to hear you call this place home?"

"My home is wherever you are," Kota whispered against my lips. "Can we take the plant with us?"

I snorted. "You don't want to get a dog or something?"

"Let's start small. The Christmas cactus is kinda our thing. We'll include it in our stories on social media. We don't want to make rash decisions—bringing a dog into our relationship might be too much too soon." Kota winked and bit back a smile.

"True. We've probably done enough moving quickly lately." I kissed him. "Yes, we can take the plant with us."

Kota glanced over his shoulder at the Christmas cactus before turning to me with a wicked gleam in his eyes. "I think we need to make sure Genevieve gets a good show from now until our trip so she's well-prepared and healthy for traveling."

I threw my head back and laughed. "Who says the plant is a female?"

Kota scooted from my lap and stripped naked before stretching out on the blankets as my mouth went dry. "First, names don't make a gender. Second, you know a lot of middle-aged women get turned on by two men having sex. But I'll take the critique." He tapped a finger against his chin. "The plant is named Genevieve-Jack, has no gender, and uses the pronoun *they*. They're all about voyeurism and their life-source comes from watching a certain sexy silver-fox suck and fuck his boyfriend within an inch of his life."

Still laughing, I shed my clothes and crawled between Kota's spread legs. "Boyfriend, huh?"

"Well, we've known each other barely a month, I think we should hold off on fiancés at least until New Year's," Kota teased as his hips rocked up, seeking. "Give Genevieve-Jack something to look forward to."

"Noted." I leaned down and kissed him until we both broke away, breathless. "It's totally weird to be purposely having sex in front of a plant."

"Probably less weird than knowing a cat or dog is watching." Kota ran his hands down my back and gripped my ass. "It's time for my boyfriend to put on a show."

I snorted, but rocked my hips, pressing our hard cocks together. "My boyfriend is bossy."

"Your boyfriend loves you and wants your cock buried in his ass," Kota murmured at my ear.

I growled and fumbled behind our blanket couch for the lube we'd left there last time.

Genevieve-Jack got one hell of a Christmas Day show.

EPILOGUE
KOTA

One Year Later

"Merry Christmas," Vince whispered against my mouth before delving his tongue inside to dance with mine. He tasted of coffee, syrup, and the load I'd just blown down his throat.

"Merry Christmas, indeed," I said as I pushed at his chest, encouraging him to stretch out on the couch so I could straddle him. Luckily, Mary Joy had finally returned the furniture to its rightful place.

After slicking his cock and my ass with lube, I reached behind me to guide his rock-hard shaft to my entrance. Sinking down on Vince's cock never got old and I gasped and whimpered into his neck as we worked together to sheath his thick length in my ass.

"Fuck, Kota," Vince growled. "Always so tight and hot." He gripped my hips.

We had exactly one hour before Mary Joy would be showing up and I had no plans on my grandmother getting a show.

Fucking for a plant was one thing, letting your grandmother see your ass getting plowed was something else altogether and I planned to avoid it.

I rode Vince's cock, loving the bite of his fingers on my hips as he pumped hard and fast into me. "Go hard, wanna feel you pump your cum deep inside."

Enjoying every second of the ride he gave me, I clenched my ass around his cock and reached back to play with his balls right before his thrusts faltered and he groaned. Loving the way his cock pulsed in my ass, I leaned down to kiss him as he filled me with his release.

"I love having sex with you no matter where we are, but there's just something about fucking you at home that makes it all that much better," Vince mumbled, wincing as I shifted and let his spent cock slip from my body.

"Home is where the heart is and I'm so damn glad to be back here for a while," I said as I pulled him to stand. "We need to clean up before Mary Joy arrives. She's bringing that new guy from Juniper Java. It's so weird to think of her dating, but she seems happy."

"I can't believe his name is Michael Joseph. Leave it to Christmas magic to bring a new guy to town with the same initials as your grandmother and have them make a connection."

I snorted. "They connected when Mary Joy marched down there to see what all the fuss was about. '*That man* wants to try to compete with me over baked goods? He doesn't know what he's getting into,'" I mimicked my grandmother's voice. "She was so pissed."

"It was the perfect enemies-to-lovers storyline," Vince said.

I winced. "Can we *not* talk about my grandma having sex?"

Vince laughed and smacked my ass. "Gotcha. Kota prefers to *not* discuss his grandma getting boned."

"Oh my God," I yelped and chased Vince to the bathroom. "Stop it. No one wants to think about that. Turn on the shower, I want to stand under the spray until it runs cold."

"This water heater lasts a very long time," Vince said.

"Exactly."

We'd been on three month-long road trips in the past year and I was more than happy to be back home instead of living out of an RV. Don't get me wrong, we'd had an amazing time and the trips had been *well* worth it, but there was just something about being in an actual house with hot water that lasted longer than five minutes.

Thanks to the road trips, I had a good supply of sleds, pallets, and several other items we'd picked up along the way for my creating. Posting our road trips to social media had slowly gained me a shit-ton of followers and my art was definitely selling more.

Of course, Genevieve-Jack's Instagram following was going to pass mine within just a few days. It was weird how many people liked to see a plant travel the country. Probably no weirder than thinking a plant was alive and healthy because we had sex in front of it.

Often.

My art business was thriving. *Kota Christopher Scott Creations* or *KCS Creations* now supported me and allowed me to live my dream of making a living creating art. Even if Mary Joy had expected me to pay rent, I'd have been able to live off my artwork.

It helped tremendously that I got paid from a few of my social media accounts. Mary Joy also sold my stuff at the Amaryllis—some customers drove to Holly Hills *just* to shop my pieces which was *crazy* to me. Mistletoe on Main, Ivy's

Grocery, and Juniper Java all let me set up sales displays as well.

Vince's contact, Martin, had been a huge part in getting my work spread out at small, specialty boutiques across the country. *KCS Creations* was known for unique, creative, one-of-a kind type art. My biggest seller was a handmade greeting card set featuring Genevieve-Jack. Each set was hand-drawn and I only made a limited number to ship to the specialty shops each month. We were working on a plan to continue with the hand-drawn sets while also making a Genevieve-Jack card set we could produce in bulk for those who weren't as concerned about one-of-a-kind.

My newest venture—one I was super excited about—was venturing into the greeting card art world. *KCS Creations* and Genevieve-Jack would remain the same, but I was happy to be designing artwork for a big-name greeting card company under the name of *Kris Scott* after my grandfather.

After showering, we dried off and dressed in preparation of Grandma's arrival. She'd insisted on bringing the entire meal and since we were having a heatwave of fifty-three degrees on Christmas Day—definitely no snow to keep us locked up this year—we'd agreed that Mary Joy could drive herself over and bring the food along with Michael Joseph. For an eighty-one-year-old, the woman was damn energetic and determined.

Vince said it was because she was getting laid.

I refused to think about that.

"I read your latest article," I said as Vince and I set the table. "You did a great job."

He'd started freelance writing for various art publications —he was very good at what he did and seemed to find a lot of happiness in writing those pieces.

"Thanks. It was a fun topic." Vince placed four glasses

around the table. "Are we doing our gifts with them or by ourselves?"

"We've got time if you want our gifts to be just us."

Vince nodded. He reached into our junk drawer and pulled out a card. "I hope you like it. Once again, it's kinda for both of us."

I opened the card.

Kota,

I fell in love with you over a year ago and I've fallen for you a little more each day. I adore our time together—whether at home or on the road—and I'm so damn proud of you for following your dreams. I feel blessed to be on this journey with you and I hope this gift will allow our adventures to be a little more comfortable. There's nothing in the world I'd rather do than travel the country with my husband in our new RV.

Love, Vince

I gasped and held up the photo of a shiny new RV. Turning to Vince, I choked back a sob of laughter when I found him on one knee.

"Oh my God, what have you done?" I whispered, my hand to my lips.

"Kota, what we have goes beyond engagement and marriage. Our love has never been one to be restrained by expectations and norms. Whether we ever have an official ceremony or just wear each other's rings and know in our hearts that we're the real thing—together forever—I wanted you to know how much I love you." Vince reached for my hand and slipped a brushed silver band onto my finger. "Kota, I want to road trip with my husband. Will you marry me?"

I sobbed out a yes and pulled Vince to his feet. "You are so damn crazy. I can't believe you bought us a new RV."

He shrugged. "I had money socked away for a rainy day."

With a trembling hand, I stealthily reached into my

pocket and pulled out the black and brushed silver band I'd been carrying around for weeks as I pushed on his shoulders and guided him to the living room. "My present for you is by the window."

Vince walked to where the canvas was leaning next to Genevieve-Jack. As he faced the window and picked up the canvas, I dropped to my knee.

I waited as he studied the four-panel piece of work. A springtime drawing of two men surrounded by green buds on trees as we walked through an outside art exhibit on our first road trip. A summertime image of us, hand-in-hand, as we wandered a trail through a tulip festival on our second RV adventure. A scene filled with fall colors and two men in an apple orchard during our third trip of the year. And an image filled with holly and lights as two men embraced, rings glinting on their fingers.

I knew the moment Vince realized what was going on and I smiled as I waited for him to put down the canvas and turn around.

When he turned to face me, I took his hand. "There is absolutely no one I'd rather take this journey with than you —even in an old RV. You beat me to the punch, but I wasn't going to be shown up. Vince, I've loved you in one way or another since you rescued me from the snow and hauled my ass up to Holly Hills. You've brought so much to my life and I can't wait to see what each season brings us from here on out." I slid the ring onto his finger. "Will you spend a lifetime of Holly Hills Christmases with me?"

Vince brushed a tear from his eye and pulled me to stand before cupping the back of my head and crushing his mouth to mine. "You're the only person I could ever imagine spending every single Christmas with for the rest of my life."

We were still in a haze of happiness when Grandma and her boyfriend walked into the living room.

"What did we miss?" Mary Joy asked.

"Just a little Christmas magic," I said with a grin before Vince kissed me and we held up our ringed fingers as Mary Joy gasped with delight.

THE END

ALSO BY A.D. ELLIS

The Perfect Blend- A steamy, M/M age-gap, marriage of convenience, coffee shop romance

Perfect Timing is a steamy, M/M romance with an introverted, demisexual writer and a big, soft teddy bear of a nurse trying to navigate a love they've always dreamed of but most definitely weren't expecting.

Adore (Remington Place 1) is a steamy, age-gap, bi-awakening, dad's best friend M/M romance with a sassy smartass and a sexy silver fox. It's the first book in the Remington Place series and can be read as a stand-alone.

Crave (Remington Place 2) is a steamy, friends-to-lovers, fake relationship M/M romance with a virgin nursing student and a gruff, grumbly construction worker.

Desire (Remington Place 3) is a steamy, age-gap, hurt/comfort M/M romance featuring a heart-of-gold mechanic and a twink who's a lot stronger than he realizes. *Please note: This story has mention of sex trafficking and sexual abuse.*

Yearn (Remington Place 4)- a steamy, enemies-to-lovers, forced proximity M/M romance between two EMS workers who have hated each other for a decade.

Power Struggle is a steamy M/M, age-gap, forced proximity romance set in a small town. A twenty-year history, rival schools and jobs, and a hotel with only one bed make for a hot and heavy, sweet and sexy, HEA-guaranteed love story.

Take Me Home M/M age-gap, opposites-attract romance with plenty of steam and a scene that will make you appreciate camouflage and work boots

Let Love In M/M age-gap, forced proximity, dad's best friend, bisexual-awakening romance. Available on AUDIO!

Let Love Win M/M brother's best friend romance. Available on AUDIO!

Buried Secrets Romantic suspense stand-alone title. Available on AUDIO!

Silver in the City (3 books- meet the Silver crew you read about in Forged in the City) Available on AUDIO!

Forged in the City (3 books- a spin-off series from Silver in the City) Available on AUDIO

The BJ Boys Series (3 books, small town, big love) Available on AUDIO

Forever Better Together (friends to lovers) Available on AUDIO!

His Reluctant Cowboy (age gap, opposites attract, cowboy romance) Available on AUDIO!

What Blooms Beneath (LGBT Fantasy romance) Available on AUDIO!

Sawyer

(this was the first M/M I wrote and you may remember Sawyer and Luke being mentioned in Barrett & Ivan as well as in Ryker & Gavin)

The Something About Him series has been revamped with revised stories, updated blurbs, and spiffy new covers.

The series is available on ALL of your favorite book platforms!

Bryan & Jase

Brody & Nick

Barrett & Ivan

Braeton & Drew

Ryker & Gavin

Kade & Cameron

A.D.'s first stories (all male/female except <u>Sawyer</u> which is male/male) are in the Torey Hope and Torey Hope: The Later Years series. Find the 8 book box set HERE or you can find each individual title on Amazon.

For Nicky

Because of Beckett

Christmas in Torey Hope

Loving Josie

Decker

Sawyer

Zach

Kendrick

ACKNOWLEDGMENTS

It's always so hard to write this part because I'm worried I'll forget someone without meaning to.

Readers- you are the reason I write. As long as you continue reading my stories, I'll continue writing them. Thank you for your support.

Bloggers- your support, reviews, and promotion are very much appreciated. Thank you!

My author buddies- I don't know that I could keep doing this without our brainstorm sessions, laughter, road trips, meals, wine, and friendship as my support.

Thank you to my alpha readers, betas, editors, proofreaders, and ARC readers! Your eyes and input are beyond important to me.

Brett and Gage- as usual, I doubt you even grasp how much your support, input, and friendship mean to me. This author journey has brought many wonderful things into my life, and you both are two of the BEST! I'm blessed to call you friends.

My family and friends- thank you for your love and support, always.

ABOUT THE AUTHOR

A.D. Ellis is an Indiana girl, born and raised. She spends much of her time in central Indiana as a teacher/instructional coach in the inner city of Indianapolis, being a mom to two amazing school-aged children, and wondering how she and her husband of almost two decades have managed to not drive each other insane. A lot of her time is also devoted to phone call avoidance and her hatred of cooking.

She loves chocolate, wine, pizza, and naps along with reading and writing romance. These loves don't leave much time for housework, much to the chagrin of her husband. Who would pick cleaning the house over a nap or a good book? She uses any extra time to increase her fluency in sarcasm.

Sign up at http://www.subscribepage.com/ADEllisNewsMMRomance for a FREE male/male romance book.

Find all of my books at Amazon- https://www.amazon.com/A.D.-Ellis/e/B00K0YJ8CW

Follow my website http://www.adellisauthor.com or find me on Facebook

http://www.facebook.com/adellisauthor

Check out my TikTok- https://www.tiktok.com/@adellisauthor

You can also find me on Twitter http://www.twitter.com/ADEllisAuthor